"It's okay. You're safe now."

Trent's arms slipped around her and he pulled her against the hard plane of his body. Against muscle and strength. She leaned back against the length of his body, trying to get as close to his warmth as she could.

She closed her eyes and soaked in the sensation. She remembered this. The moments in Trent's arms. The lingering shadows of sweet memory. But her memories paled in comparison to having him here now. Surrounding her. The scent of him. The feel of him. The solid reality of him.

She could fight memories. She couldn't fight this. She didn't even want to. She needed him too much. Needed his warmth. Needed his strength. Needed him to make her safe. Make her whole.

Dear Harlequin Intrigue Reader,

Welcome to a brand-new year of exciting romance and edge-of-your-seat suspense. We at Harlequin Intrigue are thrilled to renew our commitment to you, our loyal readers, to provide variety and outstanding romantic suspense—each and every month.

To get things started right, veteran Harlequin Intrigue author Cassie Miles kicks off a two-book miniseries with *State of Emergency*. The COLORADO SEARCH AND RESCUE group features tough emergency personnel reared in the shadows of the rugged Rocky Mountains. Who wouldn't want to be stranded with a western-born hunk trained to protect and serve?

Speaking of hunks, Debra Webb serves up a giant of a man in *Solitary Soldier*, the next installment in her COLBY AGENCY series. And you know what they say about the bigger they come the harder they fall.... Well, it goes double for this wounded hero.

Ann Voss Peterson takes us to the darkest part of a serial killer's world in *Accessory to Marriage*. The second time around could prove to be the last—permanently— for both the hero and heroine in this gripping thriller.

Finally, please welcome Delores Fossen to the line. She joins us with a moving story of forced artificial insemination, which unites two strangers who unwittingly become parents...and eventually a family. Do not miss *His Child* for an emotional read.

Be sure to let us know how we're doing; we love to hear from our readers! And Happy New Year from all of us at Harlequin Intrigue.

Sincerely,

Denise O'Sullivan
Associate Senior Editor
Harlequin Intrigue

ACCESSORY TO MARRIAGE
ANN VOSS PETERSON

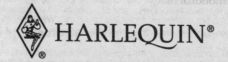

HARLEQUIN®

TORONTO • NEW YORK • LONDON
AMSTERDAM • PARIS • SYDNEY • HAMBURG
STOCKHOLM • ATHENS • TOKYO • MILAN • MADRID
PRAGUE • WARSAW • BUDAPEST • AUCKLAND

ISBN 0-373-22647-0

ACCESSORY TO MARRIAGE

This edition published by arrangement with Harlequin Books S.A.

® and TM are trademarks of the publisher. Trademarks indicated with
® are registered in the United States Patent and Trademark Office, the
Canadian Trade Marks Office and in other countries.

Visit us at www.eHarlequin.com

Printed in U.S.A.

ABOUT THE AUTHOR

Ever since she was a little girl making her own books out of construction paper, Ann Voss Peterson wanted to write. So when it came time to choose a major at the University of Wisconsin, creative writing was her only choice. Of course, writing wasn't a *practical* choice—one needs to earn a living. So Ann found jobs ranging from proofreading legal transcripts, to working with quarter horses, to washing windows. But no matter how she earned her paycheck, she continued to write the type of stories that captured her heart and imagination—romantic suspense. Ann lives near Madison, Wisconsin, with her husband, her toddler son, her border collie and her quarter horse mare.

Books by Ann Voss Peterson

HARLEQUIN INTRIGUE
579—INADMISSIBLE PASSION
618—HIS WITNESS, HER CHILD
647—ACCESSORY TO MARRIAGE

Don't miss any of our special offers. Write to us at the following address for information on our newest releases.

Harlequin Reader Service
U.S.: 3010 Walden Ave., P.O. Box 1325, Buffalo, NY 14269
Canadian: P.O. Box 609, Fort Erie, Ont. L2A 5X3

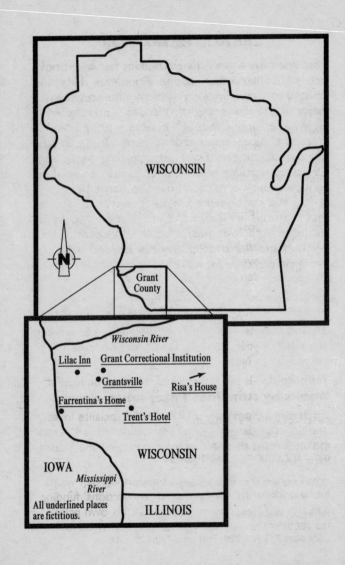

WISCONSIN

Grant
County

Wisconsin River

Lilac Inn   Grant Correctional Institution

Grantsville

Risa's House

Farrentina's Home

Trent's Hotel

WISCONSIN

IOWA   Mississippi
River

All underlined places
are fictitious.

ILLINOIS

CAST OF CHARACTERS

Risa Madsen—When her sister falls into the hands of a serial killer, Risa must do everything in her power to save her—even rely on the man who broke her heart.

Trent Burnell—An FBI profiler, Trent left Risa to protect her from the evil of his world. But when that evil resurfaces in the form of Dryden Kane, Trent has no choice but to stay and fight. For himself. And for Risa.

Dryden Kane—A brutal serial killer bent on destroying those who have tried to destroy him.

Dixie Madsen Kane—A troubled young woman looking for love, Dixie believes she's found her soul mate in Dryden Kane.

Pete Wiley—The bitter sergeant has it in for Risa and the FBI. How far will he go to prove his point?

Duane Levens—The bulky prison guard was on duty the night Dryden Kane escaped. Does he have something to hide?

John Rook—Is the police chief trying to be helpful, or does his interest have a more sinister purpose?

Farrentina Hamilton—The wealthy socialite loves the titillating danger of corresponding with a killer in prison. Would the thrill be even greater if she helped him get out?

Paul Hanson—The pompous prison warden wants his share of the Department of Corrections' funding pie and prestige. Would he sabotage his own prison to get it?

To the accessories in my marriage:
Carl and Gil Voss, always my biggest fans.
And Ellie and Pete Peterson,
thanks for raising my romantic hero.

Prologue

Do you take this woman to be your lawfully wedded wife...

Slamming on the brakes, Risa Madsen threw open her car door. She clambered out and raced through the parking lot toward the looming perimeter fence of the Grant Correctional Institution. Her heels pounded on the pavement in sync with the drumming of her pulse.

She had to stop this marriage from taking place. She couldn't—wouldn't—let Dixie throw her life away. She had to save her little sister.

And she was running out of time.

...to have and to hold...

The early afternoon sun glinted off strands of razor wire lining the top of the perimeter fence. Risa shivered as she ran. If it wasn't for her, Dixie never would have sought out Dryden Kane. She never would have transferred her exhausting need for male approval from her father to Kane. She never would have become Kane's willing victim.

...from this day forward...

Two guards stood at the gate. Stopping, Risa gulped air and struggled to subdue her panic. She focused on the bulky guard whose eyes held the look of a soul weary with confronting the evil of life. "Duane. Am I too late?"

"They already started, Professor." He opened the gate and pulled her inside. "What took you so long?"

"Traffic. I got here as soon as I could." If it hadn't been for Duane's call, she wouldn't have made it at all. She wouldn't have even known about the wedding.

He motioned for her to follow. "Hurry."

Risa ran up the steps behind him. He threw open the door and led her through a metal detector and into the wide entrance hall of the prison's main building.

...for richer or for poorer...

While a female guard patted her down and checked the inside of her shoes and the bottoms of her feet, Risa inhaled breath after breath of stale air into her hungry lungs. There never seemed to be enough air inside these walls. Nor enough light.

The perfect place for a man like Kane to live out the rest of his days.

Of course that was a thought she could never voice. In light of her profession, she was supposed to be supportive of Kane's efforts toward rehabilitation. She was supposed to believe that through psychoanalysis he could overcome his horrible childhood and turn his life around. A part of her even wanted to believe it. But she couldn't shake the cold feeling slithering over her skin every time she thought of his ice-blue eyes, his artful smirk.

The feeling of impending doom.

She knew where the feeling was coming from. Trent had planted this bias in her mind when he'd profiled Kane for the FBI. When he'd testified at Kane's trial. When he'd helped put Kane in prison.

Everything always went back to Trent.

…for better or for worse…

She shook her head, trying to dislodge the litany of vows scrolling through her mind. She had to make it to the chapel in time. She had to prevent this travesty from taking place.

Security checks complete, she hurried after Duane. Barred doors slid open in front of them and clanged shut behind. Risa's heart slammed against her ribs. She wanted to push past Duane and race for the chapel as fast as her feet would carry her. She wanted to grab Dixie and drag her out of this godforsaken place, kicking and screaming if need be.

She wished she could change the past. She wished Dixie wasn't the needy, vulnerable girl she was. She wished she had never added Kane to her list of case studies. But wishing wouldn't help Dixie. Only getting her out of this place, away from Kane would do that.

…in sickness and in health…

Finally Duane stopped in front of a plain steel door

marked Chapel. "I hope to God you aren't too late. For your sister's sake." He pushed the door open.

Risa squeezed past him and lunged inside.

Her sister stood in the corner of the chapel. Her bleached hair fell to her shoulders in platinum ringlets. At least fifty yards of lace and satin and frothy tulle flourished around her like French creme frosting. Her lipsticked mouth rounded. Her penciled brows arched in surprise. "Risa."

Risa looked past Dixie and focused on the groom. The man was charming, almost boyish, with an endearing shyness and a down-home smile. Looking at him, one would imagine him to be a kind and gentle man, the perfect husband for a troubled girl like Dixie. But Risa knew differently.

Dryden Kane was a brutal serial killer.

She strode up the aisle toward her sister, toward Kane. Her hands hardened into fists by her sides.

Kane's ice-blue eyes met hers. A smirk slithered over his thin lips. "Hey, sis. You here to welcome me into the family?"

A cold finger traveled up her spine.

"No?" His smirk grew wider. "Why not? Don't tell me you're jealous of your little sister. Do you hear that, Dix? She's jealous of you."

Dixie gazed up at him, beaming as if he'd just given her the prize of a lifetime.

Nausea swirled in Risa's stomach. She wanted to think all men were redeemable. Curable. But looking into Kane's emotionless blue eyes, she just couldn't buy it. No, Trent was right. A man like Kane never changed. He manipulated. He terrorized. He killed. But he never changed.

And he'd found just the right ploy to manipulate her sister.

Kane leered down at Dixie as if she were a roasted leg of lamb seasoned just the way he liked. "Face it, sis. Dixie has triumphed where years of psychotherapy failed. Her love has made me a better person. A good person. She's my soul mate. And you're too late to change it now. We already said 'I do.'"

The breath left Risa's lungs in a whoosh.

Kane raised his eyes to meet hers and lowered one eyelid in a profane wink. "Dixie is my wife—*until death do us part.*"

Chapter One

Risa stared at the images flashing on the ten-o'clock news. Razor wire glinting in the sun. A fenced compound. An empty cell. The newscaster's voice thundered in her ears like a death sentence. Her worst fear had become reality. Dryden Kane had escaped from prison.

Dixie.

Her throat constricted. The way Kane had leered at Dixie on their wedding day a month ago pounded at the back of her eyes. His taunting voice echoed through her mind. *Until death do us part.*

Kane would go straight to Dixie. And once he had his hands on her, he would kill her. Of this Risa had no doubt.

She scrambled to her feet and raced for the kitchen, her robe billowing out behind her. She'd been ready for bed when the terrifying story had come on the news. Now sleep was out of the question. Not until Kane was behind bars. Not until Dixie was safe. She grabbed the phone from the kitchen counter. Fingers shaking, she punched in Dixie's number.

One ring...two rings...

She clenched the phone so tightly the plastic creaked. "Please, Dixie. Please be there."

Three rings...four...

She threw down the phone and ran for the foyer, for the staircase leading to her bedroom. She had to get dressed. She had to find her purse, her car keys. She had to reach her sister before Kane did.

Her bare feet slapped the wood floor. She took the narrow steps two at a time, knocking the teddy bears decorating the stairs out of her way as she ran.

The doorbell's chime echoed through her little bungalow.

She stopped dead at the sound. Her breath caught in her throat. Was it Dixie? The police?

She raced back down the stairs to the front door. She peered through the peephole. Her heart stuttered then seized. Clutching her robe closed with one hand, she unlocked the dead bolt and yanked the door open.

Trent scrutinized her from the darkness, his face all sharp angles and hard planes in the yellow glare of the porch light.

Risa's heart started again, pumping hard enough to break a rib. She hadn't seen him in two years, two long years, and she'd never dreamed she would be glad to see him again.

But she was.

His steel-gray gaze skimmed her face. His glower deepened. "You know, don't you?"

A fresh surge of panic swelled up inside her. There was no time to lose. "I heard it on the news. We have to reach Dixie."

"Damn. I didn't want you to find out that way."

She shook her head with frustration. The way she'd found out wasn't important. "We have to reach Dixie before Kane does. He'll kill her. I know he will. We have to hurry. She didn't answer her phone."

Trent paused. His gaze drilled into her.

Cold dread penetrated her bones. He knew something. Something she hadn't seen on the news. Something horrible. She opened her mouth, but her voice wouldn't work.

Trent reached out and grasped her arm as if preparing her for the blow. "Dixie's with him," he said. "We think she helped him escape."

Risa's head whirled. Oh God, Kane already had Dixie. He'd duped her into helping him escape, and now he had her. *Until death do us part.* Risa's knees wobbled and she felt herself sinking.

Trent pushed his way into her house. Leading her to the antique bench in the foyer, he shoved teddy bears aside and deposited her on it.

Her mind stuttered. She shook her head and struggled against the pressure of his hand, the certainty of his pronouncement. No. It couldn't be true. If Kane had Dixie, she was as good as dead. "Dixie can't be dead. She can't be. She just—"

"Rees." His sharp baritone cut through her denials. He leaned over her, his face close to hers. "We don't know that she's dead. I don't think she is."

Her heart leaped at the hope in his words. Trent knew Kane better than anyone. That was why the FBI had sent him here. To find Kane. To save Dixie. "Then we have to find her. Now." She struggled to stand.

Trent's grip tightened, keeping her planted on the bench. "We will find her. But first I need you to get dressed. A police officer from Grantsville is on his way to pick you up. You need to go with him to the police station and answer some questions."

"Grantsville?" Risa recognized the name of the small town a stone's throw from the prison, but for the life of her, she didn't see how going to the tiny Grantsville police station was going to do any good. "I don't have time. We have to find Dixie. We're running out of—"

"Rees. Look at me."

She forced her eyes to focus on his face. A face full of strength and confidence and purpose. A face that, until a few minutes ago, she had never wanted to set eyes on again.

His gaze pierced her confusion like a well-honed blade. "I will find Kane, Rees. I did it before, and I'll do it now. I'll do everything in my power to bring Dixie out of this alive. I promise you that."

Trent's promises. She closed her eyes, blocking the sight of him. His riveting eyes. His hard, determined chin. God knows, he had broken promises to her in the past. But those were personal promises. Promises of marriage. Promises of a family. This one had to do with his work. This one was life and death. He would keep this one. He always kept his professional promises.

She opened her eyes and drew in a deep breath. "What will you do?"

"After the officer gets here, I'll head to the prison. I want to go through Kane's personal things, anything he left behind. Anything that will give me an idea of where he's going and what he's planning. Afterward I'll meet you at the police station. The task force will be assembling there."

"I'm going with you to the prison."

Familiar shadows crept into the gray of his eyes. He straightened and turned away, as if to prevent her from seeing too much.

"I can help, Trent. I have insights into Kane that might be useful."

He shook his head. The prismatic light from the fixture overhead played on silver threads sprinkled through his hair, making them sparkle like stars in a black night. "Go with the officer. Answer his questions. That's how you can help. There's no reason for you to go to the prison."

She tightened her mouth into a determined line. "The police will be at the prison too, right? I can answer questions there. I *need* to go."

He paced the length of the tiny foyer before he

spun back to face her. His expression was guarded, his jaw clamped shut like an oyster with an entire pearl necklace to protect.

Old anger kindled inside her. She'd seen this look countless times before. Back when they were engaged to be married. Back when he'd withdrawn. Back when he'd shut her out of his life.

She shoved her resentment aside and concentrated on keeping her voice calm, her argument reasonable. "I've been heading up a study on criminal psychology. I've been to the prison dozens of times in the last year interviewing Kane and others. I have insights into—"

"I can't invite you into the middle of a manhunt for a serial killer. Even if your sister is with him. It's out of the question."

Frustration pulsed at the back of her eyes, rapidly turning into a throbbing headache. They didn't have time to argue about this. Dixie's time was running out. Risa lurched to her feet. Her robe flared open, revealing her boxy flannel nightshirt, but she didn't care. "Damn it, Trent. You've used victims' family members to help in other cases. I know you have."

"Not this time. Let the authorities take care of it. Let us do our jobs." His voice was hard, final. But something soft hovered in his eyes. Something familiar. Protectiveness.

She balled her hands into fists. She wanted to pound them against his chest. She wanted to grab the lapels of his suit and shake him. She wanted to scream until she had no breath left in her body. Instead, she gritted her teeth, remembering his words the night he'd broken their engagement. The night he'd shredded her dreams.

Insight stabbed into her, sharp as a well-honed blade. She shook her head. "Unbelievable. You still think you're protecting me from the ugliness of the world, don't you?"

His back stiffened. Regret flickered in his eyes, but he didn't argue with her. He never had. From the night he'd told her he couldn't go ahead with their vows, he'd taken all the anger she'd thrown at him as if it were his penance for the pain he'd caused her. A punishment he knew he deserved.

But accepting punishment was beside the point. She didn't want to punish him. She wanted him to understand. "I don't need your protection. I've already met Kane. I've talked to him, interviewed him. And Dixie found my work so fascinating, she married the man, for crying out loud. I'm neck deep in the ugliness. I'm probably as tainted as you believe you are."

A muscle worked along his jaw. "You might think you are, but you're not. Not yet. And I won't be responsible for your getting in any deeper. I'm not taking you with me."

She bit back the caustic reply she wanted to hurl at him. Obviously words wouldn't do any good. She would have to take matters into her own hands. Dixie needed her. And she wasn't going to let anyone—

especially not Trent Burnell—stand in her way. "Fine. I'll drive myself to the prison. If the officer wants to ask me questions, he can meet me there. Or he can arrest me." Clutching her robe closed, she ran up the stairs.

DAMN.

Listening to the soft thump of Rees's footsteps climbing the stairs, Trent ran his gaze over the warm wood and creamy white walls of her foyer. Her collection of teddy bears scattered the staircase and bench and stared down at him from an ornate shelf. Their glossy black eyes twinkled knowingly in the overhead lights. He pulled his gaze from the bears, his skin prickling as if dozens of real eyes watched him, studied him, judged him.

Double damn.

He didn't know how he'd hoped the meeting would go, but this wasn't even close. That Rees wanted to help save Dixie from Kane—that she *needed* to help—didn't surprise him in the least. But he'd hoped she would be satisfied with going to the police station and answering questions. He should have known better.

Simply answering questions wouldn't be enough for her. Not Rees. Of course she would try to talk him into including her, and when he refused, she'd go barreling in on her own. He should have seen it coming. He should have done something, anything to

head her off before she'd latched on to the idea of
going to the prison. Before she'd dug in her heels.

He opened the door and stepped out onto the stoop.
The gentle glow of the moon caressed an oak tree's
emerging leaves and sparkled off drops of dew in the
well-tended lawn. Sweet scents of lilac and honey-
suckle mixed with the tang of nearby spruce. Familiar
smells of Wisconsin spring that would be embedded
in his memory forever.

But in his memory, those sweet scents were impossible to separate from the hot odor of blood, the
stench of decay and the evil of Dryden Kane.

That was the reality of his life. Death and decay
and a killer on the loose. Not manicured lawns. Not
teddy bears.

And certainly not someone as wholesome as Rees.

He closed his eyes, trying to shut out the soft,
lavender scent of her, the rich, husky quality in her
voice, the petite curves even that flour sack of a nightshirt couldn't hide.

Damn. *He* had brought Dryden Kane into her life.
He had infected her wholesome existence with evil.
If it wasn't for him, she wouldn't have pursued the
job at the University of Wisconsin, she wouldn't have
gone out of her way to include Kane in her study,
and her sister wouldn't have married the monster and
helped him escape.

He had contaminated her life. And now her sister
would probably die at Kane's hands. And Rees's
world would crumble.

Guilt wrenched his shoulders and pounded at his skull. If only he had never taken the job in the FBI's criminal profiling unit. If only he had never made that first trip to Wisconsin to search for the unknown subject who was kidnapping and killing coeds. If only he had never crawled into Kane's twisted mind, become obsessed with the labyrinth he'd found and become as tainted as Kane himself. He and Risa would be married now. And her sister would be safe.

But ''if only'' didn't do him a damn bit of good. He couldn't change the past. And even if it were possible to travel back in time and relive those early days, he couldn't change the decisions he'd made. To change the path his career had taken would mean killers he had helped put in prison or on death row would be free. Free to take more innocent lives. And he couldn't live with that. Not for the sake of his own personal happiness. Not even for Rees.

He stepped off the porch and strode across the wet grass toward his rental car. He couldn't go back in time, and he couldn't change things. All he could do was his job. All he could do was find Kane before he killed Dixie, before he killed someone else.

And he would do his damnedest to protect Rees in the process. Whether she liked it or not.

FINALLY DRESSED in slacks and a cotton sweater, Risa stepped into the garage and hit the glowing button on the wall. Motor whirring, the automatic garage door slowly lifted. A car's headlights glared from outside, the light growing as the door lifted, banishing the darkness in the garage. She held up a hand to shield her eyes from the light.

"Get in the car, Rees." Trent's voice barked over the drone of the garage door. "I'll drive you to the prison."

She gripped her car keys in one fist, the pointed edges digging into her palm. So Trent had changed his mind. Wonders never ceased. But knowing Trent, his decision to take her to the prison had less to do with a change of heart than a change of strategy. No doubt he'd decided he could censor the ugly truth more easily if he was with her.

Well, the first step was getting him to take her to the prison. Now she had the forty-minute drive there to convince him that she didn't need his protection, and that she could help.

She stepped out onto the driveway and punched the code into the garage door's outside keypad. The door humming shut behind her, she pulled open the passenger door of Trent's sedan and lowered herself into the bucket seat.

His scent closed over her like warm water. A shiver shimmied up her back. A shiver with a chaser of memory. Memory of a time when she'd found comfort in his scent, in the warmth of his body next to hers. But that time was gone. Gone like the love they'd once shared. The future they'd once planned.

She ground her teeth, anger winding into a tight ball in her belly. Good. She preferred anger to the simpering wistfulness and sadness of dwelling on what she'd lost. And how Trent had betrayed her. Anger kept her sharp. Focused. Determined. All of which she needed if she was to help Dixie.

Trent threw the car into reverse, backed out of the driveway and piloted the vehicle in the direction of the highway. His face was hard in the glow of the dashboard light, his eyes shuttered, as if he was bracing himself for the arguments bouncing around in her mind and had already resolved not to pay them heed.

Of course, he probably did know what she was thinking. After all, they'd first met when she was still a grad student and he was a raw FBI recruit. And God knows, eight years of courtship was plenty long enough for him to learn how her mind worked.

And how determined she could be.

She set her chin. "I need to know what is going on, Trent."

"Rees…" The muscle along his jaw clenched. His eyebrows turned down in warning. "I don't know anything beyond what I've already told you."

"And you wouldn't share it with me if you did."

"No, I wouldn't."

She blew a frustrated breath between pursed lips.

"What do you expect? Do you expect me to give you all the gory details?"

"The gory details are my *life* this time. Dixie's—" She cut off her sentence. She might as well save her breath. It was just as she'd figured. He was willing to take her to the prison, but only so he could keep her from gathering information on her own. She knotted her hands into fists in her lap. "Do you think it's better if I find out about the case when some true-crime author writes a book about it? Is that when I should discover I had the critical piece of information that could have found Kane? That could have saved Dixie's life?"

His shoulders tensed, and the ever-present shadows settled deeper in his steel eyes.

"Is it, Trent?"

For the first time since she'd climbed into the car, he turned to look at her. A furrow dug between his brows, and his face looked thinner than she remembered. Drawn. Troubled. His mouth tensed, but he said nothing.

He knew her, yes, but she also knew him. And she knew where that troubled look came from. She knew about the sense of responsibility that shrouded his heart. "I would never forgive myself if something that I know could save Dixie's life. Or other lives. Would you, Trent? Would you be able to forgive yourself?"

He flinched as if she'd slapped him. Eyes hard, he turned back to the road, his lips flattening into a noncommittal line.

She leaned toward him and laid her hand on his arm. "Let me look at Kane's things. Let me find out if anything sparks a memory of something he told me, something Dixie may have told me. Let me help. Before it's too late."

He heaved a weighted sigh, the shadows in his eyes deepening. "We'll see."

Exhaling, she leaned back in her seat and stared out the window at the rolling hills whipping by in the night.

We'll see.

It wasn't exactly a promise. But it was far more than she'd realistically hoped to squeeze out of him. And she'd take what she could get. For Dixie's sake. And for her own.

Chapter Two

Trent put pen to paper and scrawled his name on the document in front of him without glancing twice at the fine print. He knew what the document said. He'd had to sign it many times in his years with the FBI. Sign it and surrender his gun. Every time he'd ventured into the cell blocks of a maximum security prison. The bowels of a prison. The pit he and Rees were heading to now.

He glanced at Rees standing next to him in front of the glassed-in reception and screening desk. She clutched the pen in shaking fingers. She'd conducted interviews at the prison, but he doubted she'd been deeper than the visiting rooms. She would have had no reason to visit the cell blocks themselves.

Eyes squinted, she studied the words in front of her. Damn ominous words. Words she should never have to contemplate. In a nutshell, the document stated that should some inmate with a point to prove take either of them hostage, the prison authorities wouldn't lift a finger to save their lives. No negotiation. No discussion. No kiss goodbye.

Of course Trent had seen countless instances where prison officials went to all lengths to save a hostage. The document was simply intended to cover the prison from lawsuits should a visitor get hurt. But even so, the implication was there. This was a bad place filled with bad men.

A place he didn't want Rees anywhere near.

He pulled his gaze from her, from the fear and vulnerability evident in her trembling fingers and her ramrod-straight posture. He wished to hell he didn't have to put her in this situation. That he could shutter her away and keep her safe. But she'd been right. He needed to use every resource at his disposal to stop Kane, even if that resource was Rees. He couldn't live with himself if he didn't.

He turned to the hulking corrections officer waiting to escort them to Kane's cell. The sooner they sorted through the cell, the sooner he could get Rees out of this godforsaken place. And the sooner he could track down the serial killer. "Let's get on with it."

The guard nodded and turned to Risa. "Ready to go, Professor?"

Risa looked into the guard's weary eyes and forced a brave smile to her lips, a smile that trembled slightly at the corners. "Lead the way, Duane," she said, her voice a little too chipper, a little too eager.

The guard returned her shaky smile with a reassuring one of his own and started down the well-worn main hallway. Trent strode behind, Rees falling into step beside him.

"Before we reach the cell, I want to warn you." Trent projected his voice above the bars clanging behind them and the steady tap of their footsteps on scuffed tile.

"Warn me about what?"

"I don't know what we're going to find in Kane's cell. Probably what he wants us to find. And Kane is one twisted bastard. You may have to face some very ugly things."

She set her chin and strode forcefully forward. "I'll manage."

"I hope so." He didn't even bother to censure the doubt in his tone. "Because I'm bringing you along against my better judgment."

"You have to use every tool at your disposal, Trent. To save Dixie's life. To save other lives."

"That's the only reason you're here, Rees. Believe me. If I could, I'd toss you over my shoulder, haul you back to the car and hog-tie you so fast it would make your head spin."

She shot him a hard look. "If you did, there would be hell to pay."

He tore his gaze from her and strode down the corridor behind the guard's hulking shoulders. "There's always hell to pay. Believe me."

After walking for what seemed like an eternity, Duane stopped to turn his key in the control panel and opened the last set of barred doors at the entrance of the first cell block. They stepped through, and the doors clanged shut behind them. The sound echoed through the vast two-story structure like the slamming of the doors of Hades.

Trent had never visited this particular prison before, but it was much the same as the countless others he had. A long hallway stretched on either side of them, barred windows black with night on one side and two stories of cells on the other. The scarred bars and dingy beige walls and floors looked like something out of a nightmare. A smattering of murmurs, shouts and catcalls erupted as they stepped forward into the cell block. Thankfully, it was the middle of the night. Otherwise the jeers and obscenities would be worse. Much worse.

Rees tensed beside him. He longed to slip a comforting arm around her, to press her body against his side, to protect her from the scum leering at her from behind barred doors. But this was not the time or the place. That time and place didn't exist. Not anymore.

Between the open shower rooms in the center of the structure, a steel staircase rose to the second floor. They followed Duane up the stairs, their footfalls making the metal hum like a tuning fork.

When they reached the second tier, Duane led them past two uniformed police officers and down the walkway overlooking the floor below. The cells in this section stood unoccupied, evacuated, their doors yawning wide and cavernous. Trent exhaled with relief. At least Rees wouldn't have to face the prisoners' jeers up close and personal.

Two men in suits stood outside Kane's cell. The taller of the two wore a double-breasted Armani suit and French cuffs with the pomposity of a man eager for people to think more of him than he thought of himself. If Trent had to hazard a guess, he'd peg the man as the prison's warden. Though where he'd come up with the cash to dress in designer suits on a prison warden's salary, Trent couldn't answer.

The other man he knew, though not well. Pete Wiley had been one of the senior detectives on the case the last time they'd met—back when Kane was still an unknown subject, or "unsub" as they were usually called. Unfortunately, the detective had been one of many local law enforcement officers that Trent ran into in his work who were resentful of the FBI. To put it mildly, Wiley hadn't been the model of cooperation between agencies.

Now the blond mop-topped detective shifted from scuffed loafer to scuffed loafer like a little kid itching to go out and play. Or, if Trent remembered the squirrely cop correctly, an adult suffering from nervous tension and too much strong coffee.

The warden shook his balding head dramatically. Though he was talking to Wiley, his voice carried down the row of empty cells. "...and maybe this is for the best. Maybe now the Department of Corrections will give us money for improvements and extra guards instead of funneling all the state's resources into the new Supermax and into shipping prisoners to Tennessee and Oklahoma prisons.''

For the best? He hoped the warden was referring to something trivial like the boiler failing or the maintenance crew running out of wax for the dingy floors. He surely couldn't be talking about the escape of a serial killer as being *for the best,* could he? Trent eyed Rees. The last thing she needed to hear was that some jackass in a fancy suit thought the danger Dixie faced was *for the best.*

Hands balled into fists by her sides, she glowered at the warden's back. A muscle worked in the smooth column of her throat, as if she was doing her best to swallow the damn fool's words.

Anger churned in Trent's gut. She shouldn't have to swallow this garbage. Any of it. And he sure as hell wasn't going to just stand by and watch it happen. ''What the hell is *for the best?*''

The men spun around as if to pinpoint the question's source. A wary smile broke across Wiley's face. ''Special Agent Burnell.'' He nodded in Trent's direction then turned his baby blues on Rees. His brows lifted in surprise and then lowered, as if he recognized her and disapproved of her presence.

''This is Risa. Risa Madsen,'' Trent informed him.

''I know who she is.''

Trent raised his brows at the detective's hostile tone. Strange. As far as he knew, the two had never met, and yet Wiley behaved as though he held something against her.

After more introductions, the warden shook Trent's hand and then grasped Rees's. "I'm sorry your sister was involved in this, Ms. Madsen."

"Thank you, Warden Hanson. I appreciate it. Now I'm wondering the same thing as Trent. What were you talking about when we arrived? What is for the best?" She nailed him with a challenging stare.

Trent almost smiled at her pluck.

The warden's face flushed pink. "Not for the best, exactly. That was an unfortunate choice of words. But something big had to happen to get the DOC to acknowledge our funding problem. Heaven knows, they haven't been listening to me."

He gestured widely with his bony hands, his face animated. "I hold the lack of funding responsible for Kane's escape. I warned our state representative just last week we were short money for overtime and to update security."

He frowned and shook his head sadly, but no amount of acting could hide the I-told-you-so gleam in his eye. "The state legislature can't ignore the problem any longer."

Anger rumbled in Trent's chest. What a pompous fool. How could he be so insensitive as to even hint he was celebrating the extra funding Kane's escape would bring? He glowered at the warden. "With Kane on the loose, more innocent people will die. In comparison, I can't dredge up much sympathy for your prison's funding problems, Warden."

At least the pompous money grubber had the decency to appear ashamed. "Yes, of course. I was just looking for the silver lining."

"There is no silver lining that I can see." Trent glanced down at his watch. They had already wasted enough time on the warden. Time they didn't have. "Let's get on with this, Wiley."

The warden shot Trent an annoyed look and smoothed a hand over the front of his suit coat. "Yes. You'll have to excuse me. I have some administrative details to attend to. Good luck, Special Agent Burnell. Professor Madsen."

"Thank you," Trent said pointedly. He turned from the retreating warden and toward the cell.

Wiley stood in the cell's open doorway, glaring at Rees. "Why is *she* here, Burnell?"

He leveled Wiley with a no-nonsense stare. "Do you have a problem with Ms. Madsen, Wiley? As a professor of psychology—someone who has studied Kane intensely—and the sister of Kane's accomplice, she will provide insights that will be valuable. Now let's get on with this."

Trent couldn't help catch the grateful look Rees shot him. A grateful look he hardly deserved. Some nice guy he was, letting her in to see whatever gruesome surprise Kane had left for them. He could only hope she *did* have some valuable insights. He could only hope he wasn't exposing her to this whole damn nightmare for nothing.

Wiley's frown deepened, but he led the way into

the cell. Rees and Trent followed him inside. The guard who had escorted them remained by the door.

Kane's cell was small and nearly barren, with a built-in cot on one wall, a storage unit on the other and a toilet with a sink above on the third. The hall had smelled a little like sweaty gym socks, but Kane's cell reeked of something harsh and slightly minty. "Disinfectant. Kane has been up to his usual compulsive cleaning, I see."

Rees piped up from beside him. "He talked about it often. He cleaned his cell several times a day. He also said he found nothing as clean and pure as fresh, flowing blood." Her voice quavered with the memory.

Trent clenched his teeth at the tone of fear in her voice. Damn. Cleanliness was only part of Kane's compulsion. Only part of the fantasy of control he lived each time he killed. The main part of Kane's fantasy—the vital part—was the fear he caused in his victims. Their panic as he chased them through the woods. Their screams as he plunged in the knife.

The bastard would have relished the fear in Risa's eyes when he'd talked about clean, flowing blood. He would have devoured it. And hungered for more.

What the hell had Rees thought she was doing interviewing Kane? Why had she left herself open?

He knew the answer before he'd finished asking himself the question. She'd wanted to understand why Trent had withdrawn from her while working on Kane's case. Why he'd broken their engagement a short time later. And she'd gone to Kane to find the answers.

He'd delivered her right into Kane's waiting arms.

And now he was about to bring her deeper into the sordid labyrinth. Deeper into Kane's twisted mind. Deeper into the world of pain and fear and human evil.

And unless he was willing to risk lives, he couldn't do a damned thing to stop it.

He turned to the gray wooden storage structure on one wall of the cell. Comprised of shelves, cubbyholes and a writing surface, the unit was filled with stacks of letters, neatly folded magazine pages and a few trinkets. Trent glanced at Wiley. "Has anyone gone through this?"

Wiley shook his head. "When I heard you were on your way, I thought I'd better wait to get your interpretation. I certainly wouldn't want to step on delicate toes."

Trent ignored the jab and turned back to the cubbyholes. He reached in, drew out the magazine pages and unfolded them.

Rees peered around his shoulder to get a good look.

The most vile, sadomasochistic pornography Trent had seen in a long time stared back at them. A small gasp escaped Rees's lips.

Trent zeroed in on her, searching her face with a pointed gaze.

She drew herself up. Deliberately wiping all traces

of abhorrence from her face, she met his eyes. "It just surprised me, that's all."

Surprised her, hell. She knew the kind of reading material Kane favored. She hadn't been surprised, she'd been horrified. As well she should be. This kind of filth would horrify any normal person, whether she expected to see it or not. Unfortunately he'd seen more depraved things than this. And not just in pictures. The real scenes were worse. Much worse.

Rees swallowed hard and turned to the detective. "How did Kane get this...stuff?"

Wiley glanced at the pages. His mouth quirked with distaste. "It had to have been smuggled in. Probably by your sister." The venom in his voice was clear.

Trent tensed. Wiley definitely had some sort of problem with Rees. And whatever it was, he wasn't about to listen to any more.

But before he could come to Rees's defense, she nailed Wiley with a challenging stare of her own. "You obviously don't have any idea what you're talking about, Detective. Dixie would *never* have anything to do with filth like this."

Wiley shrugged. "She married Kane, didn't she?"

"Yes. She married him after he convinced her that her love made him into a better person. I doubt he could continue that charade if she saw this garbage."

So much for defending Rees, Trent thought. She could do it just fine herself where Wiley's barbs were concerned. He made a mental note to find out exactly what Wiley's problem with Rees was and directed his mind back to the real threat—Kane.

Setting the pornography aside, Trent plucked a stack of letters from one of the cubbyholes and began paging through them. He scanned each page individually, handing it to Rees when he'd finished reading.

Most were from Dixie, long opuses declaring her undying love for the serial killer, her unflagging belief in him and her bitter resentment of her older sister.

"She always has to be right, always has to be better than me... Miss Ph.D. thinks she's so smart, but she has no idea..."

Trent almost flinched at the hurtful words in the letters. Dixie was envious of Rees, that much was clear. Envy was probably normal for a troubled younger sister like Dixie. But he knew Rees wouldn't write these cruel words off as mere sibling jealousy. Not Rees. She would accept them like tender flesh accepts a sharp blade. She would internalize them. She would bleed over them.

Gritting his teeth, he kept handing her the pages.

She bit the inside of her bottom lip as she read, her expression carefully neutral, her breathing carefully even, but her eyes shone overbright.

Trent dragged his attention to the next pile of letters. To his relief, this stack wasn't from Dixie, but from a woman named Farrentina Hamilton. Where Dixie's handwriting was loopy and childish, the hand that composed these letters was pointed and bold. But save the jabs at Rees, the content of the letters was similar. Declarations of love. Promises of care packages. Plans for Kane's future outside prison—a future his multiple life sentences were *supposed* to prevent.

Trent held up the letter he was reading and focused on Wiley. ''What do you know about a woman named Farrentina Hamilton?''

''Widowed. Inherited a pile of dough from hubby. Visited Kane regularly. Several detectives are on the way to her house now.''

Trent nodded. Handing the last pile to Rees, he homed in on the trinkets still left in the storage unit. He fingered a lock of platinum hair, Dixie's probably, and a small pile of cigarettes. Then his hand moved to a stack of photographs lying facedown in one of the cubbies. He picked up the pile by the edges and turned the photos into the light. The first photo was a wedding shot of Kane and Dixie. The bride was dressed head-to-toe in frothy white, the groom in his prison jumpsuit.

Rees leaned in close to see the pictures. Close enough for him to catch a wisp of her gentle lavender scent over the sharp stench of disinfectant. Close enough to feel the warmth of her skin.

Her body tensed when she saw the reminder of her sister's union with Kane. A reminder she surely didn't need.

Trent hurriedly moved on to the next photo. The next three were snapshots of a brunette posing seductively in red lace lingerie, complete with garter belt and stockings. Uneasy tension descended over his neck and shoulders. Something was not right about the pictures. Something he couldn't quite put his finger on.

Flipping the photograph over, he read the inscription on the back. *Enjoy! Love, Farrentina.* No surprise. The seductive photos and red lace went with the bold script and contents of her letters, all right. But there was still something that bothered him.

He shuffled past head shots of several blondes, women obviously attracted to the danger and notoriety of Kane. Women he would never understand. Finally his fingers grasped the last photo.

It was a snapshot of Dixie and Rees in the foyer of Rees's home. The two of them were posed on the antique bench, surrounded with teddy bears, silly smiles on their faces.

But the photo was marred. A precise slit was cut from the locket around Dixie's neck to her thighs. Drops of something thick and dried and brown obscured her sweet smile.

Drops of blood.

Rees gasped for air and swayed into him.

Trent dropped the stack of photos on the storage unit and grasped her upper arms. Damn. Damn. *Damn.* This was just what he'd feared would happen. Kane would never pass up the chance to leave a blatant threat for whoever searched his cell.

And Trent had allowed that person to be Rees.

She trembled violently under his hands and drew

in breath after breath as if she was in danger of drowning.

He grasped her tighter, pulling her close, talking into her ear. "Rees. Remember, this is Kane's game. Manipulate, control, dominate. He guessed you'd come to the prison with me. That you'd search through his things. He put that photo there for you to find. To hurt you. To scare you. Don't let him win. Hold on to me. Breathe." He drew in deep breaths and slowly exhaled.

She followed his lead, her gasps becoming slower, more controlled until she was breathing almost normally.

He pulled back to look at her, to make sure she was all right.

Her heart-shaped face was pale as death, her dark eyes wide and glistening, but at least she wasn't going to pass out on the floor of the cell.

No thanks to him.

Anger rumbled through him. Anger with Kane. Anger with Dixie. And, most of all, anger with himself.

Rees was strong, but she wasn't strong enough to stand up to Kane's twisted manipulations. How could she be? How could any normal person face such an overt threat to the life of someone she loved? How could a normal person face such evil? "I'm getting you out of here."

She shook her head emphatically, her long dark hair lashing her cheeks. "No. I'll be all right. I—"

"Like hell you will. I shouldn't have let you come. I'm taking you back to the entrance. Now."

Ushering Rees out to the walkway, he cursed himself again for good measure. They had been through nearly everything in the cell, and she hadn't remembered one thing that would lead to Kane's whereabouts. She hadn't magically come up with the answers he was looking for. He'd risked her peace of mind for nothing.

Chapter Three

Risa leaned against one of the government-beige walls in the entrance of the prison—walls that closed in around her, crowding her, smothering her. Like all the other times she'd ventured inside the razor wire, the lack of light and air and freedom made her lungs constrict and her heart pound. But it was what she'd seen in Kane's cell that made her head throb with fear.

The sight of that photo of Dixie cut and bloody had left her shaking. She'd known Kane intended to kill Dixie since the day of their wedding, but seeing such a graphic reenactment of his earlier crimes with Dixie as his subject was almost more than she could take.

And the worst part was that he'd gotten to her. His booby trap had worked. She'd blown it. She'd insisted she didn't need protection, that she could handle whatever Kane had planned, and the truth was, she couldn't.

Trent was right. All the research she'd done into the criminal mind, all the horror stories she'd heard while compiling that research, none of it had prepared her to face the blood on that photograph. The slit down the middle of Dixie's body. The clear threat to her sister's life.

Trent hadn't thrown her over his shoulder, thankfully. But he had whisked her out of the cell block, deposited her here and instructed Duane to baby-sit until he and Wiley could gather up Kane's belongings and make sure they hadn't missed anything.

She gritted her teeth and cursed her own weakness. Thank God, she hadn't fainted. If she had, Trent probably would have shipped her off in an ambulance and ordered the doctors to sequester her in the hospital until Dixie was rescued. Or until it was too late. At least here, she could talk to the guards and do some general fact gathering on her own. She might still be able to help in some way.

She sighed and looked up at Duane. Even before he'd phoned to inform her of Dixie's secret wedding, the guard had taken her under his wing. And judging by the way he hovered over her, he was nearly as protective as Trent.

Noticing her gaze on him, Duane laid his hand on her arm, his big mitt making it look as fragile as a toothpick. "I'm real sorry about what happened, Professor."

She looked into his weary eyes. "Thanks, Duane. That means a lot to me."

The guard's coarse features clouded with obvious

anger. "Damn Kane. Why did he have to drag your sister into this?"

"I don't know." She resisted the urge to pace the floor. She didn't want to be reduced to bemoaning her sister's status as a fugitive. She wanted to *find* Dixie. She wanted to *do* something to get her little sister away from Kane.

She glanced around the entrance to the prison, at the barred doors leading to inner corridors guarded by more barred doors. Despite the warden's moans about funding for extra guards and security measures, the prison seemed awfully secure to her. Impenetrable. She couldn't imagine how a prisoner could break out. Not without inside help. "How well did you know Kane, Duane?"

Duane's mouth curled in distaste. "Know him?"

"Did you ever talk to him? Have any personal contact with him?"

Duane shook his big head. "I don't talk to the scum that lives here."

"Never?"

"Not if I can help it."

"Are any of the guards friendly with prisoners? Or more specifically, were any friendly with Kane?"

Rolling his eyes to the ceiling, he thought for a moment. "No one comes to mind."

"Can you think of anyone who would have reason to help Kane?"

Surprise registered on Duane's face. "Help him?"

"Yes. Help him escape. Someone who might have

helped him get through security and over the fence, so Dixie could pick him up."

Duane's bushy brows turned down, and he shook his head. "I think you got it wrong. He must have gotten out on his own."

"How? It seems like it would be impossible for any prisoner to get out of this place on his own."

Duane's big shoulders rose and fell in a shrug. "I can't imagine anyone lifting a finger to help a monster like that. But then I'm probably wrong. I can't imagine anyone marr—" His cheeks and neck colored with embarrassment.

"You can't imagine anyone marrying him, either," she finished for him, heaviness settling on her shoulders. "It's okay, Duane. Neither can I."

"The best thing that could happen would be if someone took Kane out while he's on the loose." His voice dropped and shadows darkened his eyes. "He didn't give those girls he killed a chance—hunting them down and gutting them like deer. Scum like that doesn't deserve to live. Not one more day. Not even if it's in a hellhole like this."

Risa barely kept herself from nodding in agreement. She wasn't a proponent of the death penalty. At least not in theory. But in this case, with a man like Dryden Kane, she could almost justify strapping him to a table and sticking a needle in his arm.

She pulled her mind from those morbid thoughts. Wisconsin wasn't a death-penalty state. And wishing for Kane's death wasn't going to find him. And it *wasn't* going to save Dixie. "Well, deciding whether Kane lives or dies isn't up to us. All we can do is help find him. Can you think of anyone at all that seemed friendly with Kane?"

Duane's forehead furrowed and he heaved a sigh as if settling deeply into thought.

Footsteps echoed through the corridor, growing louder, nearer. The barred door slid open and Trent strode through, carrying a cardboard box. Detective Wiley and the two uniformed officers who'd been outside Kane's cell followed.

She took one look at the determined line of Trent's lips and pushed herself away from the wall, standing solidly on her feet. "Did you find anything more?"

"Not much." Trent paused only to sign out at the entrance desk. When he was finished, he turned a probing gaze on her. "How are you holding up?"

The question and his tone showed nothing but concern for her, but she couldn't help feeling the heavy thump of frustration hit her in the chest once again. Frustration with herself. "I'm fine."

Trent retrieved his gun and headed for the exit. "Good. Because we're on our way to the police station."

She followed him to the door, giving Duane a parting glance.

Forehead still furrowed, the guard shot her a shy grin. "I'll think on your question, Professor. And if I come up with anybody who might have helped Kane, I'll let you know."

"Thanks, Duane." It was a long shot, but maybe Duane could tell her *something* useful. She hoped her trip to the prison hadn't been a total waste. Giving the guard a parting nod, she followed Trent's broad shoulders out into the night.

TRENT RAKED a hand through his hair and glanced at Rees. She sat slumped in a chair in the area adjacent to the tiny Grantsville police station's conference room, her eyes riveted on the polished tile floor in front of her. Her complexion was still ghostly, but at least she'd regained a little color since she'd seen the mutilated photo of her sister.

Or maybe it was just the lighting.

Another needle of guilt pricked his conscience. He'd had to let Rees examine the evidence in Kane's cell, but that didn't make him feel better about the horror she'd had to endure.

He glanced over his shoulder and into the conference room. Several file boxes sat on the long table. File boxes filled with the crime-scene photos and case reports that had put Kane behind bars the first time. At least Trent didn't have to wrestle with letting Rees see these testaments of Kane's evil. There was nothing she could tell him about these case files that he didn't already carry deep in the shadows of his soul.

He drew himself up. He had to get his mind off Rees. He had work to do and only two hours before he was scheduled to meet with the emergency task force assembled to find Kane. Two hours to come up with ideas on where Kane had gone and proactive strategies for luring him into the open.

He stepped into the conference room and pulled the door with a thunk. Turning, he faced Wiley.

The detective glanced at the closed door and arched a blond brow but refrained from comment. Good choice. If he had let one negative comment about Rees cross his lips, Trent probably would have had to throttle him.

The door opened behind him and a slightly built, dark-haired man slipped inside. He nodded to Trent, his eyes lighting up like a puppy who'd been reunited with his owner after a long absence. He thrust an eager hand forward. "Rook, sir. I'm Grantsville's Chief of Police. It's an honor to finally meet you."

Trent shook Rook's hand. The varied responses he received from local law enforcement personnel never ceased to surprise him. Most of the time his presence was met with skepticism or even downright contempt. But then there were some who saw federal agents in a much more glamorous light. Obviously Rook was among the latter group. "It's nice to meet you, too, Chief."

He ducked his head to the side, as if the title embarrassed him. "Please, call me Rook. Or John. My department has only three full-time officers, including me."

"It's about time you got here, Rook," Wiley growled. "Quit pumping Burnell's hand like some damn bootlicker and sit down. We have work to do."

Rook meekly did as Wiley ordered. Apparently the young, small-town chief was intimidated by county law enforcement.

Once they were all seated, Wiley zeroed in on Trent, waving a hand at the boxes of old files. "I looked for your profile of Kane, but I couldn't find it."

Trent stepped to the table. "There is no written profile."

"Why not?"

"We don't want a comprehensive written report leaked to the press. There are too many factors that could be misconstrued, sensationalized. Besides, we want to be able to release only select details. Details that will make the serial offender nervous. Make him take unnecessary risks. Or force him into the open. If reporters get their hands on a written report that contains the entire profile, we lose that ability."

"Reporters. We set up a media office in Platteville. Hopefully we can keep the bloodsuckers off our backs." Wiley shuffled through one of the boxes. "So do you need to make up a whole new profile? Won't that take too long?"

He didn't have to do too much to reconstruct his original profile. He saw the faces of Kane's victims in his nightmares every night. And a day didn't go by that he didn't think of them and the families they'd left behind. Think of them and curse the fear, the pain, the crippling grief Kane had caused.

Trent picked up the stack of photographs he'd

glanced through in Kane's cell. "I'll sort through the things we found in his cell and take a look at the files. I'll be ready by the time the task force gets here."

He focused on the photographs in his hands. The wedding shot of Kane and Dixie. The seductive snapshots of Farrentina Hamilton. The uneasy tension he'd experienced in the cell descended on his shoulders again. Something was definitely wrong with these pictures.

He set the photos back on the table and reached for the closest box of old case files. He plucked a file from the box, flipped open the manila folder and leafed through the contents. His fingers closed over a stack of crime-scene photos. One of the coeds Kane murdered stared back at him with unseeing blue eyes. Ashley Dalton. A twenty-year-old with two younger sisters and an interest in biochemistry. Her mutilated, naked body glowed white in the photographer's flash. Her long, blond hair tangled around her face.

He snapped the folder shut and reached for another, the haunting details of Kane's crimes rushing back to him. Rushing back to him, hell. They had never left. They were as much a part of him as his pounding heart, his straining lungs, his racing mind.

The woman in the second file was Dawn Bertram, a grad student studying psychology. A beautiful girl, Dawn had green eyes, not blue. But long, blond hair framed her lifeless face.

That was it.

That was what bothered him about the photos of Farrentina Hamilton. Her hair. Her brunette hair.

Kane preferred blondes.

Wiley leaned toward him from across the table. "What do you see, Burnell?"

Trent pushed the crime-scene photos toward him. "All of Kane's victims were blond. It was a big part of his signature. He killed blondes. Only blondes."

Rook raised his black eyebrows. "A hair-color fetish? What, was his mother blond or something?"

"Not his mother, though she probably inspired a good deal of his hatred. His rage has been building since he was a child. Rage and violent fantasies. We do know that he acted out many of those fantasies on small animals he hunted and captured in his neighborhood."

"Then where does the blond hair come in?" Rook asked.

"A few months after his mother died of cancer, he married a blonde. She was in college when they met. When she started having affairs with other men, Kane began acting out his violent fantasies on women who looked like her. Fantasies that culminated in murder. It made him feel powerful, in control. Power and control he didn't have in his normal life. Every time he killed a blond college student, he could fantasize that he was asserting power over the wife who'd humiliated him."

"Until he got around to finally killing her."

Trent nodded. He could almost smell the hot tang

of blood mixing with the scent of spruce trees and lilac bushes. Fresh blood.

Damn. If he had been a little faster he could have saved Kane's first wife. Faster identifying Kane. Faster locating him. Faster…

But he hadn't been. Kane had beaten him by mere hours.

The memory of the worried tremor in Rees's voice echoed in his ears. He looked down at the mutilated photo of her and Dixie. He couldn't let Kane beat him this time.

Wiley studied the crime-scene photos and the snapshots of Farrentina Hamilton side by side. "So he wouldn't be turned on by a brunette."

Trent snatched his thoughts from past regrets and focused on the case at hand. "No."

Wiley screwed up his forehead in concentration. "Didn't I read something in one of the Hamilton woman's letters about coloring her hair? Maybe she dyed it blond for him."

Trent skimmed through the letters until he found the one Wiley was referring to. He read aloud. *"As you can see, I colored my hair for you, Dryden. The red lingerie looks nice on a brunette, don't you think?"*

Wiley tapped a ballpoint pen on the tabletop. "But that sounds like she dyed her hair brunette for him. Not blond."

Yes, it did. But that didn't make sense. A serial killer didn't change his signature. The emotional need his crime fulfilled was always the same, crime after crime. He might change his modus operandi as he learned more efficient ways of committing his crimes, ways he could avoid getting caught. But he didn't change the emotional satisfaction, the sexual charge he got out of the act. And Kane fed on his victim's fear as he exacted revenge. Revenge against the ex-wife who'd humiliated him. The ex-wife with long, blond hair. "The sequence of this hair color change is important. Are there any other photos? Any of Hamilton as a blonde?"

Wiley flicked through the stack of photos they'd found in Kane's cell. "Yes. This head shot." He handed a photo to Trent.

Rook leaned over the table to get a glimpse.

In the picture, Farrentina Hamilton's platinum blond hair flowed over her shoulders. She wore a trendy suit, the style outdated by today's standards, and she looked appreciably younger than she did in the lingerie shot.

Damn. He didn't know what to make of this. Kane couldn't have changed his signature. But if he hadn't, why had he asked Farrentina Hamilton to dye her hair brunette?

"Dixie." Dixie was a natural brunette, like Rees, but she had bleached her hair blond for as long as Trent had known her. He picked up the wedding picture and the mutilated picture from the table. In both photos Dixie's hair was platinum and arranged in ringlets falling to her shoulders. If Kane's preference had changed to brunettes, why had he married a blonde only a month ago?

Unless Dixie, like Ms. Hamilton, was no longer blond.

Trent's gaze skimmed the mutilated photograph, landing on Rees. Her happy, wholesome smile, her arms circling her sister, her teddy bears cuddled around them on the bench. His gut tightened. "Professor Madsen might have some answers for us after all." He stood and walked to the door.

Behind him, Wiley snorted and drummed his pen on a file folder. Trent ignored his obvious disapproval.

Risa was half out of her chair before the door swung open. "Did you find anything?" Desperation tinged her voice and tightened her every muscle. She looked small, delicate among the square, government-issue furniture lining the wall. Feet rooted to the floor, she leaned toward him, straining to find answers in his eyes.

Answers he didn't have. "Will you come in here?"

Head snapping up and down in a quick nod, she scurried across the reception area and through the door he held open. As she moved into the room, his fingers stroked the small of her back as if of their own accord. The way they always had when he'd ushered her through a door. Back when the two of them were together. Back when he had a right to touch her.

The silky texture of her sweater grazed his fingertips. The warmth of her skin beckoned to him from under the thin silk.

Her body stiffened under his fingers, but she didn't look at him. Instead, she bolted into the room and took a seat at the table.

What the hell was he doing? He had no right to touch her. No right to let himself fall back into familiar patterns, familiar gestures. He'd given up those rights two years ago. Given them up to keep her safe from just the kind of evil threatening her now.

He closed the door and circled the table. Pushing away memories of holding her, touching her, he folded himself into the chair next to her.

She kept her eyes riveted to the tabletop. Following her gaze, he spotted the stack of file folders hastily shuffled together. The corner of a crime-scene photo peeked from one of the folders. The face of one of Kane's victims stared up at her. Knotted blond hair, pale skin, sightless eyes.

Trent grabbed the picture, shoved it back inside its folder and slid the stack toward Rook. As far away from Rees as he could get them. "I have some questions for you."

She looked up at him, lips drawn into a flat, tense line. She clasped her hands together in her lap, her fingers clamped tight as a vise. "Shoot."

"Has Dixie changed her hair color recently?"

Rees raised her eyebrows, clearly surprised by the question. "Yes. She changed back to her natural color."

"When?"

"After her wedding. About three weeks ago."

Wiley ceased tapping his pen for the first time since Rees had entered the room. "So she's a brunette now?"

"Her hair is about the same shade as mine."

Trent nodded. Also the same shade as Farrentina Hamilton's. "Did she say why she dyed it?"

"Oh yes. It was a big deal to her. A big compliment. She said Kane wanted her to be her natural self. He loved her just the way she was."

His stomach turned at the thought of Kane whispering those words to Dixie, his voice thick with false charm. And judging from the revulsion on Rees's face, she was fighting the same touch of nausea.

Wiley leaned forward across the scarred tabletop. "So he *asked* her to dye her hair brunette?"

"That's what Dixie told me." She glanced from Wiley to Rook to Trent.

Trent stared down at the tabletop. An icy point of foreboding pricked between his shoulder blades.

"Why do you want to know about Dixie's hair color?"

Trent raised his gaze to meet hers. "It seems Kane has changed his hair color preference from blond to brunette in the past few weeks."

She gave him a confused look.

"He asked Farrentina Hamilton to dye her hair brunette too."

"The woman in the red lingerie," she said, putting two and two together.

"Yes."

"And the women he killed before were all blond, right? That was part of his signature."

"Yes."

"So what does this mean?"

Trent blew a frustrated breath through tight lips. "That's what I'm trying to figure out. A killer doesn't just up and change his signature. It doesn't make sense. Unless..."

"Unless what?"

"Unless hair color was never really part of Kane's signature."

"What do you mean?"

He looked at Rees's long brunette hair, shining under the fluorescent lights. Hair that smelled of lavender. Hair that had once flowed through his fingers and puddled on his pillow like warm silk.

The knife of dread broke skin and delved into muscle. "Have you ever done anything to Kane that he could have misconstrued? Anything that made him angry?"

The jolt that ran through Rees's body was unmistakable.

He grasped her arm and willed her to face him. "What happened, Rees?"

She drew in a slow, deep breath. "About four months ago I published an article in an academic journal. An article about Kane, though I didn't use his name. I don't know how he got a hold of an academic publication in prison, but he did. And he figured the article was about him. He was very angry with me. He didn't like some of the things I wrote.''

"What did he do?"

"I had one more meeting with him for the book I'm working on. He agreed to see me, but whenever I asked a question, he wouldn't say a word. He'd just stare.'' She closed her eyes and covered her mouth with trembling fingers. Her face grew more pale than death.

"What else, Rees?'' he prompted.

She swallowed hard and opened her eyes, latching on to his gaze as if grasping for a lifeline. "That was when he started returning Dixie's letters. He started courting her.''

A picture formed in his mind. A horrifying picture. Dread plunged to the hilt.

Kane acted out his violent fantasies on women to serve his twisted sense of revenge. He chose victims with the same hair color as the woman he believed had wronged him. Then he played out his game— letting his victim loose in an isolated forest, hunting her down, slitting her from neck to pelvic bone. With each woman he killed, he fantasized he was asserting his power and dominance over the woman who'd humiliated him—the true target of his hatred.

And this time, he feared Kane's true target was Rees.

Chapter Four

A chill clambered up Risa's spine. She recognized the expression on Trent's face, the cloaked alarm in his eyes, and it shook her from head to toe.

Trent was afraid. Afraid for her.

Her head whirled as if the earth had been pulled from under her feet. "Trent? What does this mean?" Her whisper hung in the air, thin and fragile as gossamer. Of course she didn't have to ask the question. She knew what it meant.

Trent drew himself up, the flash of fear suddenly gone, replaced by the cool, in-control exterior she knew so well. But his calm facade did nothing to reassure her. Nothing to stop the spinning in her head.

"Kane may be fixated on you." He paused as if judging her reaction, testing how much truth she could bear. "The way he was fixated on his wife before he killed her. Before he was caught. He may be seeking revenge against you this time."

His words settled cold in the pit of her stomach. She'd seen the malevolent hatred in Kane's eyes the day he'd married Dixie. She'd heard it in the guttural undertones in his smooth voice. *Till death do us part.* And somehow, though his thinly veiled threat was directed at her sister, she'd known he meant it to hurt *her.*

It was the rest that she was struggling to accept. It was the rest that made her mind whirl and her stomach seize. "He seduced Dixie, married Dixie, and now is going to kill Dixie because of that article I wrote about him." It wasn't a question. She knew, but she didn't want to face it. She'd give anything in the world to not have to face it. "Dixie is going to die because of me."

Trent leaned toward her. His hand tightened on her arm. "You can't blame yourself, Rees. If you hadn't written that article, chances are he would have searched until he found some other way you humiliated him. And if he couldn't find anything, he would have made something up. He's the monster here. Not you."

His argument was logical. And in her mind, she knew it was accurate. But she'd learned long ago that the mind and the heart were two entirely different things. Trent had taught her that tough lesson. And right now, her heart was holding her responsible. For Kane's anger. For Dixie's abduction.

Panic rose inside her like swirling floodwaters, choking her, drowning her. "There's nothing I can do now, is there? Dixie's running out of time and there's nothing any of us can do."

"There's plenty we can do." Grasping her chin in gentle fingers, Trent turned her head to face him. "When Kane let those young women loose in the forest and hunted them down, he did it so he could make the experience last. Their fear. The kill. He wanted to draw it out. Savor it. If he kills Dixie right away, he loses his connection to you. He loses his power to torture you, to make your fear last. And that's what he wants most."

Risa closed her eyes and latched on to Trent's words, to the energy flowing from his fingertips. She wanted so much to believe him, it throbbed like a physical ache in her chest. "I hope you're right. God, I hope you're right."

Knuckles thudded against the door.

The sound traveled along Risa's nerves like a jolt of electricity. She drew in a sharp breath and opened her eyes. She was so close to the edge that any sound probably would have startled her. But the knock seemed unnaturally loud. Unnaturally ominous.

Trent dropped his hand from her chin.

Wiley snapped to his feet. She'd forgotten he and the other cop were there, witnessing her anguish. And judging from the unexplainable bitterness Wiley felt toward her, he'd probably enjoyed the show. The idea made her feel sick to her stomach. The man clearly disliked her and she had no idea why. He didn't even glance at her as he circled the table and yanked open the door. "Yeah?"

A uniformed sheriff's deputy stood outside the

door. Gaze darting to each person in the room, the deputy balanced on the balls of her feet as if poised to take off in a dead run at any moment. "We found something, Detective."

A muscle flexed along Trent's jaw. His gaze moved back and forth between Wiley and the deputy.

Wiley tossed a disdainful look in Risa's direction and gestured out the door. "In the hall."

The cop at the table sprang to his feet and followed the deputy into the hallway. Wiley brought up the rear, closing the door behind them with a decisive thunk.

Anxiety pricked Risa's nerves like a thousand tiny needles. She could only guess what the police had found, but her imagination was quick to fill in the blanks. Images crashed through her mind. Horrible images of pale skin, tangled brunette hair and blood.

Images of Dixie.

She looked to Trent, searching for answers in his eyes. Or at least compassion. But whatever emotions he might be feeling, whatever suspicions he might harbor were shuttered away from her gaze.

She should have known he would be back in perfect control. He'd slipped once by showing her his fear. He wasn't about to let it happen again. He stared past her, his attention riveted to the closed door and the conversation going on behind it.

Finally the door swung wide and Wiley alone stepped back into the room, his face a mask of calm any poker player would envy.

Trent focused on Wiley, his eyes cutting into the detective like steel-gray lasers. "What did they find?"

Wiley paused, tossing an uncomfortable glance at Risa. His mouth narrowed to a tense line.

Her blood froze in her veins. The horrible images she'd pushed from her mind came storming back. "Dixie?" she whispered. "Did they find Dixie?"

Wiley said nothing, just stared at her, his eyes hard with dislike. Maybe even contempt.

A tremor crawled up and down her nerves.

Trent stood, his tall frame towering over the detective. He shifted to the side, placing his body directly between Risa and the detective. "Damn it, Wiley, what did they find?"

"Her car."

"Dixie's car? She isn't—" Risa choked on the words.

"No, she isn't inside it. There's no body at the scene."

Risa's heart pounded against her ribs. She almost slumped over the table with relief. Maybe Trent was right about Kane. Maybe he would keep Dixie alive in order to taunt Risa. To torture her with worry. She could only hope and pray he kept her alive long enough for Trent and the police to find her. And rescue her.

Trent stepped toward the door. "How far away is the car?"

"It was found behind an abandoned barn about six miles from here."

"I'm driving out there. I want to look through it before I brief the task force." Trent turned and looked back at Risa. His eyebrows turned down and a muscle along his jaw strained as if he was waging his own private war in his mind. Finally he heaved a sigh. "Do you think you're up to going along?"

Apprehension swirled in her mind. Fear of what they might find. What they might learn. She swallowed hard and nodded. It didn't matter how she felt, how afraid she was. She had to do everything she could to save her sister. "You couldn't stop me."

Trent turned away from her and headed for the door. "I didn't figure I could."

By the time they reached the old dairy farm where Dixie's car was discovered, the birds had already started their predawn jabber. Unease and fatigue clamped Risa's shoulders like strong, merciless fingers. What she would give to be comfortable and warm and safe in her bed right now.

What she would give to have Dixie comfortable and warm and safe.

Trent piloted the car into the long driveway, tires crackling and popping over gravel. They wound their way toward the glow of police spotlights huddled around an old, once-white dairy barn.

Trent pulled the car to the side of the driveway and stopped. Switching off the ignition, he turned to face her, the glare of police spotlights behind him casting his face in deep shadow.

She squinted against the glare, unable to make out his features. But it didn't matter. She knew what his expression would be. Worried. Protective. The way Trent always seemed to look when he was around her.

"He may have left something for us, you know. A threat. A sign. Like the picture in his cell. I want you to be prepared."

She knew the dangers. But she doubted she could ever be truly prepared. Just the thought of another threat to Dixie, like the slashed photo, twisted her stomach into tight knots. But she had to see the car's contents. Because though there might be something she didn't want to see, there might also be a scrap of evidence that would lead them to Dixie. To finding her sister alive. And that was the hope she had to cling to. "Lead the way."

Trent climbed out of the car, Risa following. They moved through the handful of cops and evidence technicians toward the hulking barn. The barn's white paint was peeling like bark on a birch tree, exposing the weathered wood beneath. The gambrel roof sagged low on one side and its stone foundation was cloaked in an unruly tangle of brush. The structure had truly seen better days. A bright new sign tacked to one broad side proclaimed the farmland would soon be transformed into a neighborhood of exclusive, single-family homes.

Risa took in the barn, the sign, the bright lights and

methodical movements of the officers and evidence technicians. Yet everywhere she looked, all she saw was Dixie's face.

And the malevolent smirk of Dryden Kane.

As they walked to the center of the lights and movement, Risa spotted the flash of red paint and chrome. Dixie's Thunderbird peeked out of a bramble of raspberry bushes and twisted trunks of sumac.

Risa's heart hammered high in her chest. The car was Dixie's pride and joy. She'd saved her money for months to buy it. As if the cherry-red paint and chrome trim would make her as shiny and flashy as the car itself.

Sadness clutched Risa's heart. Sadness for her sister's lonely childhood and the needy young woman she'd become. Her first memories of Dixie were of the little girl reaching up to her daddy, begging to sit on his lap, big brown eyes turned to his, desperate for his attention, his love. And Dixie's daddy, their mother's second husband, brushing her away, too busy with more important concerns to love his little girl.

Regret rose in Risa's throat, bitter as bile. When Risa had turned ten and left to live with her father and his second wife, the move had been the best thing that ever happened to her. She only wished she could say the same for Dixie.

She shoved the thoughts of that time and the feelings they engendered back into the closet with the other skeletons and gulped in a breath of humid, spring air. The sweet scent of new grass and lilacs clashed sharply with the taste of foreboding flooding her palate. Swallowing, she clung to the sweetness. Dixie had to be out there, still alive. There had to be something in the car, some scrap of evidence that would help her find her sister.

Trent turned to her. The muscles along his jaw drew tight. His eyes drilled into hers as if digging for some evidence of hidden strength. "Ready?"

She forced herself to nod.

Trent held her gaze for several more seconds before following one of the officers to the Thunderbird's trunk. Risa followed, the thorns of raspberry bushes snagging her clothes and scratching her skin as she squeezed along the side of the car. The trunk gaped open, wide as a screaming mouth. Rounding the back of the car, she drew a deep breath and forced herself to look inside. A flowered suitcase lay alone on the floor of the trunk.

Dixie's suitcase.

Her heart lodged high in her chest for a moment and then plummeted.

Trent motioned to the suitcase. "Dixie's?"

She nodded, unable to speak, unable to do anything but stare at the suitcase and pray it didn't mean what she feared it did.

Trent unzipped the bag and lifted the flap. A jumble of clothing filled the bag, wadded as if hastily packed. Dixie's favorite ratty jeans. A flowered blouse Risa had given her for her birthday. The skin-tight capri pants that had lately become Dixie's uniform of choice. Her red vinyl cosmetics case.

A wave crashed over Risa and pulled her into the darkness like a riptide. She gasped for air, the sound sticking in her throat.

Trent's gaze snapped to her face. "Rees?"

"Her makeup case…" Blackness hung on the edges of her vision. Hopelessness. "Dixie wears makeup every day, even when she's planning to stay home and watch TV. She'd never go anywhere without her makeup case."

Trent let the flap of the suitcase fall closed and turned to look at her. "If she was in a hurry—"

"No. She would never be in that much of a hurry. He either forced her to leave it. Or…" She let her words trail off. She couldn't give voice to what she was thinking, what she was fearing. To do so would make it real. And more than anything, she didn't want it to be real.

She didn't want her sister to be dead.

TRENT'S GUT CONSTRICTED as he watched the blood drain from Rees's already pale cheeks. Before he could stop himself, he reached out and encircled her with his arms.

She pressed against him, as if he was the only thing keeping her from crumpling to the earth. Her body trembled. Her breath came hard and fast, fanning his neck in warm waves.

He tightened his arm around her and guided her

away from the car, away from the spotlights and the police and the evidence Kane had left behind. When he reached the corner of the old barn, he stopped and just held her. Held her until her shaking stopped.

He knew he should usher her out of the way, put her in the car and get her the hell home, but somehow he couldn't make his arms release her. Instead he soaked in the sensation of her body against his like parched earth soaks up rain. He'd felt her softness in his dreams. Dreams from which he'd awake covered in sweat. But this was no dream. This was the real thing. Her petite frame, the softness of her curves, her delicate lavender scent. He'd missed the feel of her, the scent of her, more than he wanted to admit.

Finally she drew a deep, shaky breath and looked up at him. Fear huddled like dark shadows in her eyes. Her normally lush lips were crimped and tight.

Cold certainty clotted in his throat. He wasn't the man to comfort her. He wasn't the man to hold her like this. The only thing he could do for Rees was to find her sister and then clear out of her life as quickly and cleanly as possible. She'd had enough to deal with. Enough worry. Enough terror. Enough heartache.

He stepped back, dropping his arms to his sides. Cool, humid air rushed to fill the space where her warmth, her softness had been. And though she was still only inches from him, the distance felt like miles. "You need some sleep. Let me take you home. I'll have the police department post an officer outside your house.''

She shook her head, setting her chin with determination. ''I can't go home. If you find anything, anything at all, I need to be here.''

The urge to reach out and pull her back into his embrace seared him like the flame of a blowtorch. He raked a hand through his hair and held his hard-fought ground. ''I'm going to be here for a while. And then I have to meet with the task force. You can't sit in on the meeting, Rees. And you'll be a lot more comfortable waiting at home than here or at the police station.''

Worry gleamed from her eyes like fever. She opened her mouth as if groping for some sliver of logic to throw out as a protest.

He held up a hand, cutting her off before the words could form on her tongue. ''Pounding yourself into the ground for no reason isn't going to help Dixie. We have some grueling hours, maybe even days ahead. You have to rest while you have the chance.''

She closed her mouth, protests unspoken. For a moment, she paused as if considering his argument. Finally she gave a reluctant nod. ''You will call me if the police turn up anything? No matter how small?''

A breath of relief escaped his lips with a whoosh. ''I agreed it would be best to involve you in this, Rees. And even though I still don't like the idea, I haven't changed my mind. I'll call if they find anything.''

"All right. Then take me home."

He grasped her elbow and ushered her toward his rental car. Even the simple touch of her elbow in his fingers zinged along his nerve endings like an electric shock. He shook his head, trying to erase the memories of her softness in his arms, the scent of her skin, the energy that pulsed from her like a life force of its own. The sooner he could get away from her, the sooner he could lose himself in his work. And, hopefully, the sooner he could find Kane and Dixie and put an end to this whole mess.

Then he could stay away from Rees. For good.

RISA LEANED BACK against the headrest in Trent's rental car and watched the lush green of Wisconsin's spring whip by the window. A weight closed in on her chest. Her arms lay in her lap, heavy, tight. She couldn't breathe. She couldn't move. It was all she could do to think of Dixie, of the chance she'd never see her sister alive again.

Kane's escape. Dixie's abduction. Trent's return. A lot to handle in a lifetime, let alone one night. The first two filled her with horror. The last with relief and fear and pain and regret.

She was glad Trent was here, for Dixie's sake and her own. But to be near him, even for one minute, was to be swamped in feelings from the past. Memories of walking hand in hand through Washington at cherry-blossom time. Feeding each other strawberry

shortcake in bed. The warmth of his strong body holding her, surrounding her, inside her.

She entwined her fingers together in her lap and
concentrated on the familiar houses of her neighborhood scrolling by the window. She had to be careful.
She couldn't let her memories of the good times
they'd had swamp her. She couldn't let her need for
his help now pull her under. She had to remember
the knife-sharp pain of losing him. And the fact that
when this nightmare was over, however it turned out,
he would be leaving her again.

When they finally pulled into her driveway, she
expected the tension coiling in her muscles to relax,
but it seemed only to wind tighter. The dawn sun
inched over the east horizon. Its rays reflected off the
front windows of her house, making them glow like
the eyes of a demonic beast.

Trent switched off the engine. His gaze scoured the
front of her house, combing the Japanese yew out
front, the shadows behind the garage. Tension seemed
to radiate from him like heat from the dawning sun.
He unfastened his seat belt and unbuttoned his suit
jacket. Reaching inside the jacket, he pulled a gun
from his shoulder holster. "I'm going to check out
the house. Stay close behind me."

Her chest tightened. She hadn't even considered the
possibility of Kane coming here, to her house. "You
think he might be here? Waiting for me?"

"I'd like to think even he isn't that bold, but I'm
not going to take the chance."

A shiver claimed her. Suddenly the risk of stirring old memories and pain by being near Trent didn't seem so dangerous. Not compared with finding a serial killer in her house. "I'm right behind you."

He held out his hand. "Keys?"

She rifled through her purse. Her trembling fingers closed over the keys' sharp edges. She fished them out and dropped them into Trent's open palm.

He turned away from her, opened the car door and climbed out in one fluid movement. She followed, falling in close behind.

Trent's footsteps clicked on the cement walk, shattering the dawn stillness. He mounted the porch steps and thrust her key into the lock. He threw open the door, hesitating a moment before stepping into the house, gun barrel leading the way. Once inside he stopped dead. His body tensed. He swung his gun in front of him, as if combing every inch of the foyer.

Something was wrong. She peered around Trent's wide shoulders.

At first she didn't know what she was seeing. White fluff seemed to be everywhere in her little foyer. On the polished oak floor, on the shelf, on the antique bench. A breeze from outside caught the fluff and swept it toward the far corner.

Her pulse throbbed in her ears. Her teddy bears. Her collection of teddy bears. They stared at her with shiny eyes, their usually round bodies depleted, empty. Slashed.

Kane.

Her head spun. Her knees wobbled.

Suddenly Trent's arm circled her. Holding her. Propping her up. Pulling her from the house. His solid chest pressed against her side. His breath rasped in her ear.

She grasped his arm, tight around her middle, and clung.

Chapter Five

Trent held Rees tight to his chest and backed down the cement walk. The soles of their shoes scraped against the cement as they shuffled backward. His pulse throbbed in his ears. He held the gun steady in his hand, his gaze combing the shadows behind the yew, the low branches of the spruce. He could feel Kane's eyes on him. On Rees. He could almost hear the monster's low, satisfied chuckle.

Kane was watching. He'd want to see Rees's reaction to the mutilated bears. He'd want to see her fear. He would feed on it. Revel in it. It would make him feel powerful.

And he'd hunger for more.

Trent clutched the gun tighter in his fist. Wasn't it enough that Kane lived inside Trent's mind, inside his heart like a black spot of death? Wasn't it enough that Kane and his ''artwork'' had stolen Trent's peace, his dreams, his happiness, his future?

Now the bastard wanted Rees's too?

Damn Kane. Damn him to hell.

Reaching the rental car, Trent guided her into the passenger seat. He slammed her door safely closed. Circling the car, he scanned the shadows of trees and bushes, the rooflines of the neighboring houses before ducking behind the wheel. The engine turned over with a flick of the key, and he shifted into gear. The car leaped to life.

He backed out of the driveway. It was all he could do to keep from stomping on the gas. He wanted to squeal tires and race down the street. But he wouldn't let Kane know he was shaken. He wouldn't let Kane see his fear. Even if it meant forcing himself to pretend he and Rees were out for a Sunday drive. That nothing out of the ordinary had just happened.

Gaze raking either side of the street, he reached for his cell phone and placed a call to Pete Wiley before they rounded the corner. The sooner the police reached Rees's house, the better. They might not catch Kane, but a fresh trail could give them the edge they needed to bring him down.

Only after he completed the call did he allow himself to glance at Rees, to look into her eyes.

Fear looked back at him. Terror. Just the effect Kane wanted.

Anger sliced Trent's composure. Images flashed through his mind. Women hunted down. Women left sprawled in the wilderness like so much trash. Women with lives and futures and people who cared about them.

He had to get Rees away from here. Far away.

Kane wouldn't get what he wanted. Not this time. Not unless he killed Trent first.

And that wasn't going to happen.

RISA COULDN'T STOP SHAKING. Not even after Trent had hustled her into his hotel room in Platteville and bolted the door behind them.

She ran her gaze over the room, the two chairs hovered around a tiny round table, the broad expanse of the king-size bed. It was an average hotel room, relying on its very commonness to make guests feel secure.

In this case, the strategy didn't work.

Everywhere she looked, she saw tufts of white stuffing blowing in the breeze. And all she felt was the chill of Kane's controlling rage.

The chill slashed over skin and stabbed into muscle. Stabbed into bone. She wrapped her arms around her middle and shivered.

She had always been able to take care of herself. And not just herself. Others, too. Even as a child, she'd watched out for her sister and mother. She'd been the strong one. The one who'd helped her mother to bed after a night of vodka. The one who'd made sure Dixie finished her homework when no one else cared. The responsible one. The one in charge.

What a laugh. Right now she felt about as in charge as a newborn baby. And about as strong. Her knees wobbled, solid as water.

Trent moved up behind her, so close she could feel

him, almost touch him. His scent washed over her, musk and male. Strong and safe. "You should sit down." His voice rumbled through the quiet room and vibrated in her chest, more a feeling than a sound.

"Before I fall down?" She tried to inject humor into her voice, but it fell flat. Instead her voice sounded small. Tremulous. Afraid.

"Yes. Before you fall down."

She nodded but didn't move. She couldn't. Not only was she unsure her legs could carry her the four or five steps to the bed, but she didn't want to move away from him. From his warmth. From his strength. "I can't. I—"

"It's okay. You're safe now." His arms slipped around her, skimming her sides and wrapping tight around her waist. He pulled her against the hard plane of his body. Against muscle and strength.

A chill spread over her skin, a chill not caused by fear. A chill that was the antidote to fear. The cure. She leaned back against the length of his body, trying to get as close to his warmth as she could.

His arms closed tighter around her. Pressing his lips to her temple in a gentle kiss, he sighed, his breath grazing the side of her face and sending several strands of her hair dancing over her cheek.

She closed her eyes and soaked in the sensation. She remembered this. The moments in Trent's arms. The lingering shadows of sweet memory. But her memories paled in comparison to having him here now. Surrounding her. The scent of him. The feel of him. The solid reality of him.

She could fight memories. She couldn't fight this. She didn't even want to. She needed him too much. Needed his warmth. Needed his strength. Needed him to make her safe. Make her whole.

Without breaking contact, she turned in his arms, pressing against him, molding her body to his. Every muscle. Every ridge. She reached up, locked her arms around his neck and pulled him to her.

His hand moved to the back of her neck, as it had so many times in the past. He cradled her head, entwining his fingers in her hair, and lowered his mouth to hers.

His lips fit perfectly. Like they always had. Like she'd known they still would. His tongue moved into her mouth, infusing her with his strength.

But it wasn't enough. Not nearly enough. Not close enough. Warm enough. Safe enough. She wanted to feel him, the hard wall of his chest, the taut muscle of his stomach, the tight ridge of his desire. She wanted to mold to him, skin to skin, no barriers between them.

She fumbled at the buttons of his shirt, pulling them free until the fabric parted under her fingers and she could slip her hands inside.

He shrugged out of the shirt and clutched her against his chest. His skin rippled warm and smooth over hard muscle. She traced the even lines of his ribs, the flat plane of his belly, the ribbon of coarse hair leading to his waistband. The feel of him was so familiar, yet new.

And she needed more. Needed more like she'd never needed before.

As if reading her thoughts, her need, he smoothed his hands down her back and grasped the hem of her sweater. He slid the cotton up, baring her skin to the cool of the air, the heat of his touch. He broke contact with her lips only to lift the sweater over her head and discard it.

Not willing to wait one more second, she reached around her back and unhooked her bra. She slid the flimsy lace garment off and let it fall to the floor.

She reached for him. She needed his heat. Needed to feel his skin against hers. Her breasts flattened against his chest, the coarse sprinkling of hair abrading their sensitive tips.

A groan rumbled in his chest. Lowering his head, he devoured her mouth, his lips nipping and caressing, his tongue demanding and giving. His fingers found the waistband of her slacks. Unbuttoning. Unzipping. He eased them over her hips and let them fall. Her panties were next. He pushed the lace down her thighs, past her knees. His actions coiled with strength and need of his own.

She held him tighter. Wanting to be part of him, to meld with him, to become stronger together than they ever could be apart.

Grasping the waistband of his slacks, her fingers

found the button, the metal tab of the zipper. She pulled the zipper down.

His trousers slid down his legs, and he kicked them free. He slipped his hands down her sides, over the swell of her hips and cupped her buttocks. Lifting her, he pulled her against his body, against the straining bulge in his briefs. She spread her thighs, wrapping her legs around him, fitting her body to him. Cupping him, holding him, rocking against him. This was what she needed, what she wanted. To feel alive. To feel safe. To feel strong.

He took the few steps to the bed, and laid her on the mattress. His body covered her. His heat seeped into her, firing her blood past fever, past reason.

Her breath rasped in her ears, harsh, uneven. Her heart pumped, strong against her ribs. She needed more of him. All of him. She worked her hands between their bodies. She slipped her fingers under the elastic waistband of his briefs. "I need you so much, Trent. I never stopped needing you."

His body went rigid. He drew a sharp breath and let it out in a shudder. "We—" His hand closed over hers and stilled. "We can't, Rees."

Pulling back from his kiss, she opened her eyes, searching his face, trying to make sense of what he was saying, why he had stopped.

His skin was flushed. His eyes echoed the want, the need she knew glistened in her own. He swallowed hard and shook his head. "We can't do this."

His words fully registered this time, slicing deep.

His skin was still melded to hers. His weight still bore down on her. But he was pulling away. Distancing himself. Denying her needs. Denying his own.

Like he had done before.

"What do you mean, we can't do this? Why can't we, Trent?" Anger pulsed like blood from the wound. "Because you're afraid of tainting me?"

His mouth flattened into a hard line.

It was a low blow and she knew it, throwing his old feelings, his old confession back in his face. Deliberately trying to hurt him. But she couldn't help it. She wanted to hurt him. Like he'd hurt her two years ago.

Like he was hurting her now.

He rolled onto his back, cool air rushing to fill the space where his body had been. "I'm sorry, Rees."

"For what? For denying me what I need?"

He closed his eyes and turned his face to the window. Soft light filtered through the sheers and glowed off the planes of his face, making the stress lines framing his eyes and mouth appear etched deep as the abyss that had opened between them. The abyss he wouldn't cross.

She blew a tortured breath through pursed lips. "If you're so sorry, then don't pull away."

Turning back to face her, he opened his eyes and clawed a hand through his hair. "It's not that simple, and you know it. Not between us."

"It *is* that simple, Trent. It's just that simple. I was stronger in your arms just now than I am alone. *We* were stronger. And *we* need that. Even if it's just for now. *We need that.*''

His brows turned down in anger and frustration. ''We need to escape the reality of Kane. The darkness. The death. But making love with me isn't going to help you do that. It's just going to bring you more pain.''

She opened her mouth to protest, then closed it without uttering a word. He was right. Making love with Trent wasn't going to help her escape the threat of Kane, the fear of losing Dixie. Needing him, melding with him, losing herself in him would only bring her pain. It had brought her plenty of pain already. But no matter the pain, she couldn't shake the feeling that she was stronger in his arms. And where did that leave her?

Her stomach knotted and her eyes stung. She rolled away from him and climbed off the bed. Forcing her knees to support her weight, she walked across the room and into the bathroom.

She closed the door and leaned against it, the solid barricade pressing along the length of her spine. She looked down at herself. At her naked breasts, nipples red from rubbing against the rough hair of his chest. At her thighs and the triangle of hair guarding the center of her passion, still throbbing from his closeness.

She grabbed a bath towel from the rack and wrapped it around her nakedness as if clothing herself with armor. She couldn't think about past pain, past regret. She couldn't dwell on what would never be. She couldn't let herself need him, want him. She had to be strong all on her own. The only thing that mattered now—the only thing that could matter—was getting Dixie away from Kane before it was too late. And she would do whatever she had to to make sure that happened. No matter what the cost.

TRENT HOISTED HIMSELF UP from the bed to sit with his back against the headboard. He punched the pillow behind him with his elbow. Damn, damn, damn.

When had he lost control of his senses? When had his sexual urges gotten so strong they eclipsed common sense?

Rees needed him to hold her, comfort her. She didn't need him to claim her lips. Nor tear off her clothes. Nor take advantage of her vulnerability. And even though he'd managed to bring himself under control before he'd really crossed the line, he'd hurt her in doing that, too.

Hurt her. Again.

He closed his eyes, pressing the pads of thumb and forefinger hard against his lids until color mushroomed behind his eyes. Rees needed his protection now more than ever before.

He knew what he was up against. He'd seen the atrocities Kane was capable of committing. The mutilated bodies. The terror frozen in dead eyes. And, God knows, he'd felt Kane's darkness stain his own soul, a stain that festered and grew until it choked out every last vestige of light.

He had to protect Rees from Kane's knife. And he had to protect her from Kane's darkness. If only Trent could manage not to wound her any more himself in the meantime.

The bathroom door swung open and she stepped back into the room. Wisps of dark hair brushed over naked shoulders and cascaded down her back. She'd wrapped a towel around herself, the pressure of the tightly wrapped terry cloth mounding her breasts above it. The bottom edge of the towel barely covered the tops of her slim thighs.

The image of her naked body, the sweet scent of her, the feel of her, was seared into his mind. Everything she'd just offered him. Everything he'd just pushed away. He stifled a groan and shifted on the bed, trying to relieve some of the pressure in his groin. Trying to calm nerves that were strung tighter than piano wire.

She set her chin in that stubborn way of hers and looked him straight in the eye. "I know how we can catch Kane."

His gut clenched like a fist. Whatever she had in mind, he wasn't going to like it. He could tell by the hell-bent-for-leather tone in her voice. He shot her a skeptical look and waited for the other shoe to fall.

"This teddy bear thing pretty much establishes that Kane is after me, right?"

"Right," he said, his voice deliberately emotionless and flat.

"And he will likely follow the pattern he did with his wife, right?"

Trent nodded. "He'll likely start killing women who look like you, same hair color, same build." Like Dixie. And though he didn't say it out loud, he knew by the flash of panic in Rees's eyes, she was thinking the same thing.

She swallowed hard as if to choke down the fear and drew a deep breath. "He'll kill other women until he works up enough excitement and anticipation to come after me."

"Right. And he won't quit. Not until we catch him…"

"Or until he kills me."

He forced a nod. Rees had it right except for one detail. Kane would never stop. He'd find another woman who had wronged him. Another woman to avenge himself against. And the whole pattern would begin again. Each time the fantasies would become more violent, his hunger for his victims' fear and pain more voracious. It would take more to satisfy him. But he would never stop. Killers like him never did. Not until they were caught.

Or killed.

Rees took a step further into the room. "Since Kane really wants me, not Dixie, why don't we use that to our advantage?"

Foreboding slid along Trent's nerves. "You're not suggesting what I think you are."

"Why not? If he really wants me, then why not use me to draw him out?"

Her suggestion tightened around his throat like a garrote. He gasped for air. "Bait a serial killer? A man as dangerous as Kane? Have you lost your mind?"

"You're always talking about being proactive. And this might work. Why not try it?"

His legs tensed with the need to climb off this damn bed and close the short distance between them. His hands opened and closed with the need to grab hold of her and shake some sense into her. "It's too dangerous, that's why."

"And doing nothing isn't dangerous? For Dixie? And for me? Trent, he's going to kill her and then come after me anyway."

He swung his legs over the edge of the bed and lurched to his feet. He wanted to say he didn't give a damn about Dixie. That he cared only about Rees. He wanted to rip off that flimsy towel, throw her back on the bed and cover her with his body. Wrap her in the safety of his arms and never let her go. But he couldn't do any of those things. He *did* care about Dixie. And his arms *weren't* a safe place for Rees to be. He'd more than proved that. "I'm not going along with this."

"You'd still be protecting me, Trent. But we might save Dixie, too. Be reasonable."

"Reasonable?" Anger spiked his blood with a shot of fire. "You're talking about dangling yourself in front of Kane like a worm on a hook, and *I* should be reasonable? Forget it, Rees."

"Dixie's running out of time." Her voice shrilled with urgency.

"I said forget it." He grabbed his trousers from the floor and yanked them on. Even if it was their only chance to save Dixie, he damn well wouldn't let Rees sacrifice herself to draw Kane out.

She pointed an accusing finger at him. "If this was one of your other cases, if I was just some woman you didn't know, you'd okay it. Wouldn't you?"

He clenched his jaw, his teeth aching under the pressure.

"Wouldn't you?" she demanded.

"I don't know. The fact is, it's *not* one of my other cases. And I won't use you that way."

Rees shook her head, her thick chocolate hair rustling around bare shoulders. Her face pinched as if she was going to cry with frustration. But she didn't let one tear fall. Instead, she snatched her rumpled clothes from the floor. The wad of clothing tight in her arms, she shot him an undaunted look. "Lucky for me you're merely assisting in this manhunt. Pete Wiley will jump at the chance to use me to draw Kane out. And there's nothing you can do about it." Not waiting for a reaction, she spun on her heel and stalked into the bathroom. The door slammed behind her with the finality of a death sentence.

Trent started toward the door, ready to do whatever it took to make her see reason. He stopped dead two feet from his destination and slammed his fist into his open hand.

Damn, damn, *damn.*

There wasn't anything he *could* do. He *was* here only to assist the local cops. He *didn't* have the final say. If she wanted to offer herself on a platter to trap Kane, he couldn't do a damn thing to stop her. Her life would be in Pete Wiley's hands. And if he read the detective's contempt for her correctly, Trent had more than just Kane to worry about.

Chapter Six

Risa stared at the closed door to the tiny Grantsville police station's conference room and chewed her bottom lip. She still hadn't been able to talk to Pete Wiley.

By the time she and Trent had arrived at the police station for the task force briefing, Wiley had already taken his place in the conference room along with nearly a dozen detectives from Grant County, neighboring counties, the state police and the couple of cops from the tiny Grantsville P.D. Even a handful of men in suits that looked suspiciously like federal agents had filed into the too-small room. She had no choice but to wait until the briefing was over to make her offer to Wiley.

Finally the door opened and detectives spilled out of the room. Rubbing sweaty palms against her jeans, Risa tried to pick out Wiley's blond hair from the small crowd.

"Professor Madsen." A young police officer headed straight for her, eyes burning with the intensity of one of her star students. She could swear she'd seen him somewhere before, but her foggy mind wouldn't supply the time and place.

"John Rook. Remember? Grantsville Chief of Police. We met in the conference room this morning, although I don't think we were ever officially introduced." His prominent Adam's apple bobbed as he talked. He stuck out a bony hand. "I have a few questions for you about your sister."

She shook his hand and looked past his eager eyes, searching the crowd. She didn't want to let Wiley sneak out the door while she was answering the police chief's questions. "I'd be happy to answer your questions, Chief Rook. But right now I'm looking for Detective Wiley. I have something urgent to discuss with him. Have you seen him?"

"Please, just plain Rook will do. Or John." He waved a hand in the direction of the conference room. "Wiley's still in there talking to Special Agent Burnell."

Great. Trent was undoubtedly giving Wiley reasons he couldn't involve her in the manhunt. Well, good luck. If she'd read Wiley's attitude toward her correctly, Trent could talk until tomorrow and Wiley would still jump at the chance to use her as a lure for Kane.

"Could we set a time to talk later? Where are you staying?" Rook looked at her expectantly.

Where *was* she staying? She couldn't go back to her house. It was a crime scene now. And besides, she couldn't set foot inside her foyer again without seeing mutilated teddy bears. Without feeling Kane's presence.

She thought of Trent's hotel room. The king-size bed. The warmth of his arms. The cold pain that sliced her heart when he'd pushed her away. And the longing that plagued her despite the lingering hurt.

Hopefully Trent would arrange for a separate room for her. "I—I'm not sure yet. I think Special Agent Burnell is taking care of the arrangements."

"Then I assume you'll be at the same hotel he is." Rook pulled a card from his jacket pocket and stuffed it into her hand. "He'll be plenty busy, so you should have time to talk with me. Give me a call anytime. And I'll be right over."

She shoved his card into her jeans pocket and smiled into his overeager eyes. Apparently Rook intended to prove his little department could solve cases right along with the much larger county sheriff's forces. Whatever fueled his ambition, she was grateful for it. She could only hope everyone else involved with the case was so eager. Dixie's life depended on it.

"I'll call as soon as I have a moment. Anything to help Dixie." Stepping away from Rook, she peered into the open doorway of the conference room just as Wiley ambled out, deep in conversation with a balding detective.

Mustering her courage, she set her chin and stepped forward. "Detective Wiley?"

His head snapped around, and he gave her a disdainful look. "Burnell's still inside." He gestured into the conference room with a nod of his head and turned his attention back to the balding detective.

She took a determined step toward him. "I need to talk to you, Detective."

A skeptical cloud settled over Wiley's sharp features.

"Alone."

He settled cold eyes on her and shook his head. "If you want information about the hunt for Kane, I'm not your boy. You go snuggle up to Burnell. I'm not some minion here to serve you, Professor." He sneered her title as if it were a derogatory word.

She stood her ground. She didn't have a clue why Wiley disliked her so much, but it didn't matter. In fact, his dislike was just what she needed. *He* wouldn't be concerned with protecting her. *He* would take her suggestion and run with it. "I want you to use me to lure Kane into a trap."

He shot the detective next to him a quick glance. "Talk to you later, Mylinski."

Lips crooking in a smile, the detective popped a piece of candy into his mouth and sauntered away.

Wiley's mouth drew into a hard line. "Does Burnell know about this?"

"Yes. He doesn't like the idea."

His gaze crawled over her. "I bet not."

She stood straighter under his scrutiny. "I'm Kane's real target. Not Dixie. Not some other innocent woman Kane might kill. So how about it? Will you use me to draw him out?''

A smile crept over Wiley's mouth, stretched into a full-fledged grin. ''You bet I will. This could be just the break we need.''

Risa stifled a shiver of fear. It was done. For better or for worse, Trent couldn't stop her now.

As if the thought of him conjured him from the mist, Trent appeared in the doorway. One of the well-dressed men with the look of federal law enforcement stood beside him. The two of them were a matched set except for the other man's more pointed features and shock of white hair. Salt to Trent's pepper.

An uneasy feeling slithered up Risa's spine.

Trent's gaze shot from Risa to Wiley and back again. His brows pinched in a frown. ''Rees, this is Vince Donatelli. He's from the Bureau. The Milwaukee office.''

The Bureau. The FBI. Her unease spread into all-out foreboding. ''And what brings you out here, Special Agent Donatelli?''

''I'm here to get your sister back, Professor Madsen.'' The man gave her a smile undoubtedly designed to be reassuring.

The grin didn't reassure her at all. And the fact that he was familiar enough with the case to know her name and title without the benefit of introduction worried her even more. She nodded her head in Wiley's direction. ''The sheriff's department is doing a fine job of that. Why would the Bureau send someone in addition to Trent?''

"The sheriff's department *is* doing a fine job." Donatelli nodded his kudos to Wiley and turned serious eyes on her. "But we received reports that Kane and your sister were seen on the Iowa banks of the Mississippi. And once he transported her across state lines, it became an FBI case."

"Someone saw—" She caught her breath. "Kane couldn't have taken Dixie to Iowa. He was at my house this morning. He shredded my teddy bears. He couldn't have gone to Iowa and come back again that fast. It's impossible."

"It's not impossible," Trent said in a low voice. "It's not even a two-hour drive from your house to the Iowa border."

She turned blazing eyes on Trent. Were Kane and Dixie really spotted across the border? Or had Trent trumped up a publicity-seeker's sighting as an excuse to bring his FBI colleagues into the case? To take control of the manhunt from the sheriff's department? To take control from Wiley?

Beside her, Wiley shifted his weight from foot to foot like a dancing prizefighter. "The professor here was just telling me how she would be willing to help us set a trap for Kane."

Donatelli raised aristocratic eyebrows. "You're suggesting using a civilian as bait?"

"I'm suggesting nothing. She offered." Wiley's voice rang with defensiveness and thinly disguised hostility. Apparently he appreciated the FBI taking over his manhunt about as much as he appreciated Risa.

Donatelli shook his head. "We won't consider that option until we've exhausted all other avenues."

Risa's head throbbed in time with her pulse. She turned her glare on Trent, clenching her hands at her sides to keep them from shaking with the frustration building inside her like a geyser ready to blow. "I want to talk to you, Trent. Now."

He nodded carefully. "Fine." Judging from the look on his face, he knew what was coming. And judging from the speed with which he excused himself, he knew exactly how close she was to losing control right here in front of Donatelli and Wiley.

"Follow me." He led her out the front door to the tiny gravel parking lot, now nearly emptied of cars. Starting for his rental car, he unlocked the doors with a press of his keyless remote. "Get in the car. We'll talk on the way."

Risa came to a dead halt. The last thing she was going to do was crawl back in that car and let him whisk her to someplace safe, far away from any chance she might have of helping track Kane and Dixie. "Damn you."

He stopped and turned to look at her, like a human punching bag waiting for the latest torrent of abuse.

"You—" She glanced around at a straggler walking to his car and struggled to control the volume of her voice. "You made up this Iowa sighting, didn't you?"

"No. There was a sighting. I just took full advantage of it."

Took full advantage of it? A nice way of saying he took a sighting no one would ever believe was real and blew it out of proportion. "And when Donatelli took over the case, you talked him into excluding me. You told him the risk was too great."

"Of course I did. The risk *is* too great."

"But I'm the one taking that risk. It should be up to me."

His mouth flattened into a hard line. "Getting yourself killed isn't going to help Dixie."

Uttering an angry growl, she shook her head and started back in the direction of the police station.

"Wait, Rees. Get in the car. You're coming with me." He reached for her. His fingers brushed her arm, but didn't close around her bicep. Instead he yanked his hand back as if it had been splattered with hot grease and let it fall limp at his side.

She stopped in her tracks, staring at his hand. "Now you're withdrawing from a simple touch?" Anger blossomed within her like a mushroom cloud. Anger over his withdrawal two years ago. Anger over his withdrawal this morning. Anger over old pain and new, mixing and swirling inside her. Searing like fire. "Are you afraid merely grasping my arm will contaminate me?"

His jaw hardened to stone. "Open your eyes, Rees.

Look what's happened to Dixie. Look what's happened to you so far. If I hadn't brought Kane into your life, you and Dixie would be busy living your lives, not in fear of losing them. I've *already* contaminated you.''

She opened her mouth to speak, but her voice caught in her throat. He wouldn't listen. He would never accept that her selection of Kane to be part of her study didn't have anything to do with him.

And realistically, she didn't accept it, either.

Kane's case had changed Trent. He'd gone to Wisconsin and returned to her a different man. A tortured man. A man who couldn't marry her.

After he'd canceled their wedding, she'd thought it an ironic coincidence when the University of Wisconsin had offered her a professorship. But when she'd started her criminal psychology project and compiled her list of prisoners to study, it was no coincidence that she'd included Kane's name. She'd wanted to know what had changed Trent. She'd wanted to find some answers. She'd wanted to look the devil in the eye.

And she had.

But it wasn't answers that she'd found. She'd found only anger and hatred and evil.

She focused on the man in front of her, the stubbornness hardening the planes of his face, the desperation in his eyes. The memory of his warm arms surrounding her, infusing her with strength tingled through her. The ache of cold air rushing over her skin as he pulled away throbbed in her heart.

She couldn't fight his logic. Not when much of what he said was true. Not when her own heart bled with each beat.

She swallowed hard. "All right, Trent. Have it your way. All of this is your fault. You contaminated me. And you should stay as far away from me as you possibly can." The words were bitter on her tongue. She spun around and resumed her march to the police station, her legs heavy as lead. If she was lucky, Police Chief Rook would still be inside and eager for their chat about Dixie. Trent might lock her out of his heart and out of his life, but he couldn't keep her from assisting in the search for Kane.

Behind her, Trent's car door slammed and the engine roared to life. Gravel popped and spit under tires as he gunned the vehicle in a tight circle and hit the brakes in front of her, cutting off her path.

He leaned across the passenger seat and threw the door open. "Get in, Rees. I'm not letting you out of my sight."

"You're not going to let me out of your sight, but you're afraid being near me will contaminate me? Don't you see the irony in that?"

He gave her a withering frown in response.

"No. I guess you wouldn't."

"Damn it, Rees. Get in the car."

She set her chin and stood her ground. "Not until you tell me where we're going."

"Back to the prison."

TRENT WATCHED Rees settle into the corner of the little interview room provided for depositions of prisoners and force herself to bite into the vending machine sandwich. Even though she hadn't eaten in almost twenty-four hours, she looked about as hungry for the cold ham and cheese on rye as he'd been. Tough. She needed something to keep her going.

Her skin had already taken on the pallor that comes from prolonged stress, and her eyes held a sheen he'd seen too many times in the families of victims. She'd been through a hell of a shock. First the trauma of Kane kidnapping her sister, and then learning she herself was the serial killer's true target. It was amazing she was still standing.

She needed food. She needed sleep. She needed comfort.

He'd taken care of the first order. But sleep would be hard to come by.

And comfort?

God knew he wasn't the man to supply that.

Images of the moments in the hotel room bombarded his brain. The sight of her naked body. The feel of her breasts pressed against his chest. The smell of her scent clinging to his skin. Lavender and woman. Passion and regret.

He shook the images from his mind. He couldn't allow himself the luxury of remembering. Not if he was going to keep under wraps the passion that had exploded between them. Not if he was going to protect her. From Kane. And from himself.

Thank God the Iowa sighting had brought Donatelli in on the case. If it hadn't, he would have had to make something up, because there wasn't a chance in hell that he was going to let Rees dangle on Wiley's hook, challenging Kane to bite.

But if they didn't get a break soon, if Kane started knifing women instead of teddy bears, Donatelli would be forced to use whatever tool he could to capture the killer. And the most obvious and effective tool would be Rees.

Trent had to prevent that from happening. He had to find something—a thread they'd missed, a piece of evidence—something to lead them to Kane before he killed again.

And that's what had brought them back inside prison walls. Someone had helped Kane escape. And the most logical place to start was with the guards.

Knuckles rapped on wood and the door swung wide. The guard who had escorted them to Kane's cell the day before lumbered into the room. Duane Levens. The harsh overhead light glared down on him, draining his face of color and adding shadows around his deep-set eyes. Eyes that flicked to Rees.

"Hello, Duane," she said.

Trent shot her a warning look. It was bad enough he had to have her sit in on the meeting. He didn't want her any more involved than necessary.

Levens offered her a shy smile before narrowing his eyes on Trent. "You asked to see me?"

Trent had chosen to start with Levens because the burly guard had seemed cooperative the first time they'd met. But judging from Levens's narrowed eyes, his demeanor seemed to have changed considerably in the past hours. Trent motioned to the chair next to him at the bolted-down table. "Have a seat."

The guard lowered his big body into the chair, his movement rigid with wariness. The man was probably pissing his pants at the thought of being questioned by the FBI after a prison break on his shift.

And Trent could use that anxiety to his advantage. He got right to the point. "It looks like Kane didn't pull off his escape all by himself, Levens. It looks like he had help. Inside help."

The tinny smell of sweat and fear tinged the air. The big man shifted in his chair. "What does this have to do with me?"

"That's what I'm asking."

A stain of red crept up the guard's neck and blossomed over his cheeks. Righteous anger flattened his mouth and turned down the inside corners of his bushy brows. "It doesn't have a damn thing to do with me, that's what."

Trent kept his expression carefully blank. "Oh?"

"That's right. I would never help a murdering bastard like Kane."

"So you would never let him into the garbage bay

right before the truck arrived to pick up the waste-paper and cardboard?''

"No.''

Trent let the guard's denial hang in the air. Most people with guilt on their consciences rushed to fill silence, as if saying nothing was an undeniable verdict of guilt.

But Levens didn't bite.

Time to work another angle. "What were some of the things you and Kane talked about in his time here?''

A fresh surge of angry color rushed to the guard's cheeks. "I don't talk to scum.''

"Kane was a charming guy. If you didn't know his background, you could almost say he was nice. Surely he chatted with the guards.''

"Not with me he didn't.''

"Never?''

"No.''

"Are you saying I could ask some of the other guards working your shift, and they would say that *not once* did they see you talking to Kane?''

He seemed to flinch slightly at the thinly veiled threat. "I never talked to him unless I had to.''

"And what did the two of you talk about? When you *had* to talk, that is?''

Levens's eyes had the look of a man being led someplace he didn't want to go. "He'd complain about the food or about being locked in his cell too long. Stuff like that.''

"And what did you say to him in those exchanges?"

An expression of pure contempt darkened the guard's eyes and curled his mouth into a sneer. "I told him to go to hell. Son of a bitch got far more consideration than he deserved. More than he gave those girls he killed." Cold hatred dripped from his voice.

Interesting. His hate for Kane seemed genuine. And strong. "So you didn't like Kane much?"

Levens reined in his emotions, his face returning to the wary mask. "No."

Trent eyed the big guard. Time to shake him up a little. See if he could derail him. He snapped open his briefcase and pulled out a thick file that had nothing to do with the prison or Levens. A small fact the guard would never know. Laying it on the table, Trent tapped the closed manila cover as if the file contained all the damning proof he could ever need. "It seems Kane has been receiving special favors, more time out of his cell, phone privileges, that sort of thing. And he received virtually all of those favors during your shift. Can you explain that?"

Levens lurched forward in his chair. "I don't care what that file says. I didn't give Kane anything. The only thing I wanted to give him was a bullet in the head." The guard slammed his fist down hard on the table. His hatred for Kane hung in the air like noxious gas.

Not the type of behavior a man who'd helped Kane

would display. But that didn't mean he didn't have an inkling about who *had* helped the serial killer. "If not you, where were these favors coming from, Levens?"

"I don't know."

"One of the other guards?"

"I don't know. I can't help you. Now leave me the hell alone, and let me go back to work."

Trent leaned toward the guard. "I need answers. If you don't give them to me, I'll have to get them from someone else."

"Then get them. I'm out of here." Levens shot to his feet.

"Wait, Duane," Rees implored from her corner.

Trent tensed at the sound of her voice and gave her what he hoped was a silencing glare.

Levens stopped in his tracks and turned to her.

"I know you hate Kane," Rees said, her voice steeped in understanding. "You never would have tried to help me stop Dixie's wedding if you were helping him."

The guard nodded, tilting his chin at a self-righteous angle. "Damn right."

"But someone helped him escape. And that someone could know where he is." She rose from her chair and walked across the small room to Levens's side. She reached out and laid a hand on the big guard's arm. "I need your help, Duane."

Trent wanted to tell her to sit down, to stay out of this. He wanted to shuttle her straight back into her corner. But her voice had stopped Levens in his tracks. And her plea was softening the wariness in the big guard's eyes. Trent bit his tongue and waited to see what would happen next.

Rees continued in her soft voice. "Who do *you* think would have helped Kane?"

Levens shook his head. "I truly don't know, Professor."

The warden's enthusiasm over additional funding as a result of Kane's escape rang in Trent's ears. "What about the warden?"

The hulk's eyebrows shot toward his hairline. "The warden? Why the warden?" His eyes darted to Trent and narrowed, as if he'd suddenly realized where the question came from.

Rees picked up the ball Trent had tossed out. "When we met the warden outside Kane's cell this morning, he complained about funding shortages at the prison, remember? About not having enough money to pay guards overtime wages, or to update security measures. Are his complaints legitimate?"

Levens bobbed his head in a nod. "We're always short staffed."

"What about updating security?" Rees continued.

"I don't think one thing has been updated since I started working here. And that was ten years ago."

Rees glanced at Trent, as if she'd run out of questions.

Trent thought back to the warden's specific complaints. "He mentioned that the prison's funding was being diverted to out-of-state prisons and to the new Supermax penitentiary.''

Levens let out a guffaw. ''Yeah, I thought that was a good one.''

A slight smile turned up the corners of Rees's lips as if she was dying to be let in on the joke. ''What's so funny, Duane?''

''It's not the funding that the warden has his shorts in a bundle over.''

''Oh?'' Trent raised his brows and waited for the guard to explain.

''The Supermax is a real thorn in his side.''

''How so?'' Trent prodded.

Levens shot him a condescending look, as if the answer was more obvious than dirt. ''Look at this place. It's falling down around our ears. It's the biggest dump in the state system. It's no secret Warden Hanson took the job at Grantsville as a stepping stone. He wanted to head the Supermax.''

''But he was passed over?''

''Not only that. Some of his most notorious prisoners are being transferred to the Supermax next week.'' A bitter smile tweaked the guard's mouth. ''All the warden will have left is crumbling walls housing a bunch of no-names. Not much to brag about at cocktail parties.''

Levens's words shifted and fell into place in Trent's mind. The funding issue. The lost promotion. The prisoner transfer. A picture was forming. A picture that reeked of revenge—Hanson's revenge against the

DOC for a long list of slights. There was only one piece missing. A piece that would tie the entire package together. "Kane is on that list of prisoners scheduled for transfer, isn't he?"

A deep furrow cut into the guard's forehead at the use of Kane's name. Hatred once again chilled his eyes. "Yes."

Chapter Seven

Trent pulled the car into Warden Hanson's driveway. Throwing the car into Park, he studied the house cowering beyond the spiked security fence. Long shadows of approaching twilight fell over the house, but lights glowed from inside. Someone was home. Good.

Hanson had already left work when they'd finished with Levens, but Trent couldn't afford to wait until the next morning to question him. There was no telling exactly when Kane would strike next, but Trent was willing to bet it would be soon.

Very soon.

He glanced at Rees, sitting by his side in the dim car.

Catching the look, she turned a bitter smile in his direction. "You're welcome for the help with Duane."

The sarcasm in her voice thudded into him like a kick in the gut. Her help had been invaluable in questioning Levens. But it was still help he didn't want. Not from her. She was already over her head in this mess. He sure as hell didn't want to draw her in deeper. He'd already drawn her in deep enough. "If you're expecting me to thank you, don't hold your breath."

"Don't worry. If I had started holding my breath where you're concerned, I would have turned blue and died long ago."

He said nothing. There was nothing to say. Nothing that would take away her frustration. Nothing that would erase her hurt and anger. Anger he knew he deserved.

All he could do was focus on Kane. On people who might have helped the serial killer escape and those who might know where he was now. Because he sure as hell couldn't focus on Rees. On the memories. On her scent wafting toward him in the still night air. On the sensation of having her by his side. If there was anything he couldn't afford to think about, it was that.

"Stay here." He threw the door open and climbed out of the car. A security phone was nestled on one side of the gate. Interesting. It seemed Hanson not only had a penchant for expensive suits, he also tended to go overboard on security for his home. He picked up the phone and pushed the Call button. A light shone down on his face, illuminating his features for a security camera's eye.

"Who's there?" a woman's voice squeaked from the phone.

"FBI, ma'am," Trent announced. "I need a word

with Mr. Hanson. It's about the escape from Grantsville prison.''

Silence answered him, heavy as the humid night
air. Finally the voice erupted again. ''How do I know
you're really FBI?''

Trent held his badge up to the camera lens. ''I'm
Special Agent Trent Burnell, ma'am.''

''Someone else is there, too. Who's with you?''

He glanced over his shoulder. Rees moved up close
behind him, into the camera's view. The light scent
of lavender rode the air.

He'd been so distracted by his thoughts, he hadn't
heard her get out of the car and approach. But he was
aware of her presence now. Too aware. He groaned
inwardly. He should have known she wouldn't stay
put. ''Professor Risa Madsen. She's assisting me in
the case.'' He forced the words past his lips, cringing
inwardly.

Though he didn't look in her direction, he felt Rees
smile. No doubt she loved *that* explanation of her
presence.

''I'm sorry.'' The thin voice rose again from the
phone, snapping his attention back to the matter at
hand. ''Paul isn't home.''

''Do you know when he'll be back?''

''No.''

Trent frowned into the receiver. She didn't know,
or she wasn't going to tell? ''Is this Mrs. Hanson?''

The phone line deadened with silence.

''Ma'am?''

"Yes," the voice fluttered.

"May we come in and talk to you?"

"No, I—" She drew a shaky breath. "I'd rather not let anyone in. Not while Paul is gone."

If she thought she was going to get rid of him that easily, she had another guess coming. "This is an urgent matter, Mrs. Hanson. I really need to talk to you."

"I'm not comfortable having visitors while Paul is out. He'll be at the prison tomorrow. You can talk to him there. Please."

Unease pricked the back of Trent's neck. He studied the tall security fence, the drawn draperies of the house beyond. If he'd needed another reason to stay away from Rees—to call off their wedding—this was it. He could never have borne the idea of Rees being sentenced to a life of fear and paranoia because of the evil pervading his life. The kind of existence that apparently, Mrs. Hanson was living. "Are you all right, Mrs. Hanson?"

"All right? Oh, yes, I'm fine. I'm just not comfortable inviting you in. There are so many bad people out there. So many people who do horrible things. I'm just not comfortable." Fear quivered in her voice.

Rees stepped closer to him, concern and questions creasing her brow. He could just imagine what she was thinking, only hearing his side of the conversation. He angled his back to her. The last thing he needed was to worry her further. "If you let me in, I can check the house for you, make sure everything is secure.''

"No. That's not necessary. I'm fine. I just don't take visitors when Paul isn't home. Please.''

The unease riding Trent's neck graduated to a sting. Was Mrs. Hanson's fear merely paranoia? Or was she afraid of something more specific? Something like Dryden Kane? Trent reached into his suit jacket and unsnapped his shoulder holster.

Behind him, Rees drew a sharp breath.

He steeled himself against the sound and forced his attention to scouring the house and surrounding landscape. "Is someone in the house with you, Mrs. Hanson?''

"What? No. I already told you I'm alone. That's why I don't want to let you in. I don't know you. You could be anybody.''

He drew in a deep breath of patience, still searching for anything suspicious, anything out of place. "I'm an agent with the FBI, ma'am. I showed you my badge.''

"How do I know what an FBI badge looks like? It could be fake. You could be one of those inmates coming after my husband. You could be anyone.''

This was getting stranger by the minute. He rubbed the back of his neck. "Have inmates come after your husband before, ma'am?''

"Well, no. But it could happen. Anything could happen. I have to go now.''

"I'm sorry, ma'am. If you don't come out to the

gate so I can make sure you're okay, I'll have to come in.''

Silence stretched across the phone line.

''Ma'am?''

''Very well. But only for a moment.''

A click sounded on the other end of the line and the phone went dead.

Trent replaced the receiver.

''What's going on?'' Rees whispered, her voice thin and frightened.

''Probably nothing.'' He couldn't help but glance at her over his shoulder. A big mistake.

Eyes dark and rounded with fear, she looked so frightened and vulnerable that it was all he could do to keep himself from taking her into his arms. He forced himself to turn away and focus on the house. ''Go back to the car and wait.''

He could feel her stiffen. And in his mind's eye, he pictured her lips pursing and her chin jutting in a stubborn angle. ''Not a chance. I'm staying right here. You can't get rid of me that easily.''

He didn't figure he could, but it was worth a try. He'd feel a damn sight better if she was in the safety of the car if anything did go wrong. And it sure wouldn't hurt to get her distracting presence as far away from him as possible.

After a long minute, the front door finally swung open and a skeleton-thin woman with long brown hair stepped onto the porch. With small shuffling steps, she approached the gate. "Here I am. Are you happy now?"

Happy wasn't the word. "I'm relieved you are all right."

"I told you I was all right." As she drew closer, the streetlight illuminated her features. Her face held the pinched pallor of long-suffered fear.

Mrs. Hanson stopped ten feet from the fence and eyed them suspiciously. "Is this about the bribes?"

Bribes? Trent tried his best not to let his surprise show. He didn't know anything about bribes, but he wasn't about to tell Mrs. Hanson that. Instead, he nodded. "What can you tell me about the bribes, ma'am?"

Beside him, Rees craned her neck toward the woman, as if straining to catch every word.

Mrs. Hanson shook her head. "Probably nothing you don't already know."

Since he didn't know a damn thing, he doubted that. "Please, start from the beginning."

She eyed him warily for a full minute before she began. "About a month ago, Paul noticed that serial killer who escaped was getting extra TV time and time out of his cell. He thinks some of his guards may have been accepting bribes. Surely he told you this already."

"Not me personally, but another law enforcement officer," he bluffed. "Did Warden Hanson tell you who he thought was paying the bribes?"

She sighed. "I overheard him talking on the phone.

The name was unusual. I can't quite recall. Farrah, or something. A woman.''

"Farrentina?"

"That's it."

Farrentina Hamilton was bribing guards. And the warden knew about it. Interesting. A vision of Warden Hanson's Armani suit and French cuffs filled Trent's mind's eye. He could guess why he hadn't mentioned bribes to law enforcement. Ms. Hamilton had a lot of money. More than enough to pay the warden for his silence.

"Well, thank you for your help, Mrs. Hanson. I'll speak with your husband another time." He eyed the frail woman, her trembling hands twisting a shank of her long brown hair. "I'll have the local police check on you."

"Thank you. I'd appreciate that. Good night, Special Agent." She nodded in Rees's direction. "Professor."

"Good night," Rees returned.

Trent watched Mrs. Hanson's fervent glances and hurried steps back to the safety of her house. As the woman closed the door behind her, Rees turned to look at him. "It's so sad."

He pulled himself from tangled thoughts of Warden Hanson and Farrentina Hamilton. He wasn't following. "What's sad?"

She gestured to the house, locked tight and shuttered behind the security fence. "Mrs. Hanson. The poor woman. It's as if she's using gates and locks to shut out everything from her life. And now all she has left is shadows and fear.''

A feeling Trent lived with every day. ''Maybe it's the only way she can do what she needs to do. The only way she can survive.''

''Then surviving is all she's doing. Because she isn't living. Not that way.''

Trent's chest ached with each beat of his heart. A life infested with evil wasn't truly living. It was only survival. The meanest, basest kind. Rees didn't know how right she was.

And if he had anything to say about it, she never would.

''READY?''

Risa nodded to Trent. Keeping her eyes locked on the cement structure jutting out of the thick bank of trees ahead, she stifled a shiver. She didn't feel ready. Not one bit. She didn't want to meet Farrentina Hamilton. She didn't want to learn what kind of woman sent erotic photos of herself to a serial killer. But if Farrentina had any knowledge of Kane's whereabouts, Risa wanted to hear it. And even though the cops watching Farrentina's expansive estate hadn't seen any sign of Kane, Risa wasn't about to hang around outside and wait.

Trent strode up the twisting walk ahead of her, his stride long and even. His suit moved with his body like a second skin, sleek and powerfully male.

Risa averted her eyes, concentrating on the cement

path under her feet, but it didn't help. She could still feel every step he took, every nuance of movement. Her body was as tuned to his as it had been when they were together.

As if they were two pieces of a whole.

She shook her head with the irony of that feeling. She couldn't afford to let herself moon over what they'd lost. Couldn't afford to let herself ache for what they'd never find again.

She gritted her teeth and pushed Trent from her mind. She had far more important things to focus on. Questioning Farrentina, finding Dixie, things she could do something about.

Reaching the stoop, Trent pressed the doorbell. Rather than a bell, a single, vaguely electronic tone echoed through the house.

"Charming," Trent muttered under his breath.

If the circumstances had been different, Risa might have smiled and added a wry observation of her own. But as it was, the corners of her mouth refused to turn up, and her voice died on her lips.

"I will be asking the questions, Rees. Understand?"

"Yes, sir." Sarcasm sharpened her voice to a point. Truthfully, she felt a little relieved. While she liked Duane and knew she had a positive influence on him, she didn't know Farrentina. And she didn't want to. A fact that surely wouldn't encourage the woman to open up.

After a minute, the light over their heads blinked

on, and Farrentina herself pulled open the massive door.

She looked older than she did in the pictures. Lines fanned the corners of her eyes and creased the edges of her mouth. Her eyes held the bruised look of someone who had seen too much. "So it's the feeb and the sister-in-law. To what do I owe this dubious pleasure?" Her voice was soft, breathy, making her flippant comments sound dissonant like swear words on the tongue of a child.

Obviously Farrentina had heard about them from Kane. Risa tensed, looking at the dark forest then back at the house. Could Kane be here? Could Farrentina be hiding him?

Trent positioned himself in the path of the door like an experienced salesman. "I have some questions I need answered."

Farrentina waved her hand in the air, the bell sleeve of the red silk robe she wore flapping like a matador's cape. "Well come in, if you must. I sure hope the two of you are more entertaining than the cops I've talked to so far." She whirled away from them and walked through the gaping foyer, hips swaying, leaving Risa and Trent standing in the open doorway.

Trent ushered Risa inside and closed the door. He scanned the foyer, every muscle on alert, as if he expected Kane to jump out at any moment.

Risa sidled a little closer to him and glanced around the foyer. White marble stretched across the floor and reached up sheer walls to the cathedral ceiling where a crystal chandelier dripped clear, sparkling light. Spotless white carpet swept up the silver-railed staircase. The scent of lemon cleaner tinged the air.

Kane's obsession with cleanliness popped into her mind. The killer would love a place like this. Empty, sterile. No doubt Farrentina knew what he liked. Had she arranged everything from the decor to the smell in the air to please him in case he happened to drop by?

Risa shivered. Drawing a deep breath, she followed Trent and the retreating red silk flourish of Farrentina Hamilton through the archway and into an adjoining room. This room wasn't much cozier than the foyer. Decked out in white walls, white carpet and white leather furniture, it had all the homey charm of an ice castle.

Farrentina crossed the room to a wet bar and brandished a bottle of premium vodka. "Drink?"

Trent shook his head. "No, thank you."

Her eyes narrowed on Risa. "You?"

Risa had guided her mother to bed too many times after a bout with the bottle to risk developing a taste for alcohol. But if there was ever a time when she understood the need for a drink, that time was now. "No, thanks."

Farrentina raised her sculpted brows, screwed up her mouth in a disdainful expression and reached for a tumbler. "Well, if I'm going to wade through tedious questions all over again, I'm going to have a drink in my hand." She glugged vodka into the glass.

After filling the glass nearly to the brim with straight booze, Farrentina crossed to a chair and sank into it. "You two going to sit or just stand there?"

Trent selected a chair facing the entrance of the room. Risa perched on the couch near him.

Eyeing them both, Farrentina raised her glass to her lips and took several unflinching gulps. Her hand trembled slightly as she drank.

A prickle of unease skimmed the back of Risa's neck at the sign of vulnerability. She clutched her hands in front of her.

Gathering her composure, Farrentina turned her attention to Trent. "So you want to know about my relationship with Dryden, right? If I've seen him? If I know where he might be? If I know whether or not he has his little wife with him? Am I on the right track?"

Trent said nothing, but merely watched her with keen interest. The glow from the room's indirect lighting cast his face in soft shadow, making him look all-knowing. The effect wasn't lost on Risa.

"Well, I don't know where he is," Farrentina blurted into the silence. Apparently the effect wasn't lost on her either. She raised her chin in an overexaggerated show of strength, as if challenging Trent to accuse her of lying. "I haven't seen him, and I assume the whiny little wench is with him, from what the police have told me."

"Did you smuggle pornography to Kane in prison?"

She crooked a sculpted brow, obviously surprised by the question. "Is that a crime?"

"Not something the FBI would be concerned about."

"Then yes, I did. What of it?"

Trent's face showed no surprise, no judgment, no emotion whatsoever. "Did you buy him favors with the guards? More time outside his cell? Extra television privileges?"

"What do you care?" She jutted her chin forward once again, but the small quiver of her lower lip belied her show of confidence.

Risa shifted uncomfortably. She focused on Farrentina's bloodred nails clutching the glass.

"Who did you pay for these favors?" Trent asked.

"Why should I tell you that?"

"I want whoever helped Kane escape. You can either cooperate and give me that person's name, or you can take the fall all by yourself. I'll be inclined to believe that person was you."

Swallowing hard, she glared at him. "If I could have, I would have helped him myself. He didn't belong in that place. He didn't deserve that kind of treatment. It was all his first wife's fault, you know. That bitch. She drove him to do the things he did. It's not fair. She's dead now. It's over. Dryden shouldn't have to pay his entire life for the grief she caused him."

Risa's stomach roiled. Farrentina had bought all of Kane's rationalizations. Just as Dixie had.

Knife-sharp pain stabbed into Risa's chest. She

pulled back from the thought. She couldn't think of Dixie now. She had to focus on Farrentina. On Trent's questions.

"Who did you pay for the favors?"

"I don't remember their names."

Trent held out a slip of paper. From where Risa was sitting, she could make out a list of names. "Which of these prison guards did you pay?"

Farrentina's eyes skimmed the list. "Caldwell, Franklin and Bollinger."

"Only those three?"

"Yes."

Risa sighed with relief. She never believed Duane would help Kane. He hated the killer through and through. But she was still relieved to know she was right.

"You and that Detective Wiley should have shared information. He seemed to know every move I made in the last year and who I made them with."

"Wiley?" Trent's voice registered the same surprise that rocketed through Risa.

How did Wiley know who Farrentina had bribed? And why had he neglected to tell Trent?

Trent wiped the flash of surprise from his face and narrowed his eyes on Farrentina. "Where did Wiley get his information?"

"Search me. I didn't tell him. And I doubt the guards I paid were broadcasting they took bribes." Farrentina tried to pull off a casual shrug, but the gesture was tight and self-conscious. "The only other person who knew was Dryden. I suppose he could have told Wiley.''

Risa almost gasped out loud. Questions bounced around in her head. Questions with an edge of panic. Was Wiley involved with Kane in some way? Was that where his hatred for her came from?

Trent angled his head to the side and scrutinized Farrentina. ''Did Kane mention Detective Wiley to you, Ms. Hamilton?''

''He talked about cops sometimes. But he never used names. He wasn't friendly with any of them, if that's what you're getting at.'' Farrentina's gaze landed on Risa. ''I'll bet your sister knew about the special favors.''

Risa's back arched with defensiveness. ''Dixie isn't involved in this.'' Even as the words left her lips, she realized how ridiculous they were.

And from Farrentina's expression, she realized the outlandishness of the claim as well. ''She married Dryden, didn't she? And she's with him now. Maybe *your sister* paid someone to help him escape. The good little wife and all that.''

Risa bit the inside of her lip. She wanted to tell Farrentina that Dixie would never pay to set a man like Dryden Kane free. She wanted to say that Dixie wasn't anything like Farrentina. But her voice curdled in her throat.

''How do you feel about Kane marrying Dixie instead of you?'' Trent's voice cut through the weighted silence.

Farrentina seemed to shrink in upon herself. Pain pinched her face. But she managed to shrug, as if she didn't care. "Dryden and I have a special bond. Something much stronger than a white dress and a piece of paper from the state."

Trent raised his eyebrows. "And what might that special bond be?"

"Chemistry." A lewd smile twisted Farrentina's mouth. But under the bravado, the poor woman's false confidence fissured and cracked like porous rock in winter. Aching vulnerability haunted her bruised eyes. "We've taken our own private vows."

Risa averted her gaze. She didn't want to see Farrentina's vulnerability. She didn't want to know the woman had a heart under that facade. A heart that could be wounded. She wanted her to be belligerent, powerful, and every bit as evil as Kane. Not a poor injured bird like Dixie.

"What's wrong with you, honey? Jealous? Dryden said you had a thing for him."

Revulsion crept over Risa's skin.

"And *he* has a thing for Risa, too, doesn't he, Farrentina?"

Trent's words brought Farrentina's attention snapping back to him. "A thing for her?" She clutched her crystal tumbler in her lap until her knuckles turned white with the pressure. "You don't know what you're talking about."

"I know Kane. Didn't he tell you? I'm the one who caught him the first time."

Her mouth tightened into a hard line. Her eyes darted to Risa and then back to Trent.

"He wants Risa, doesn't he, Farrentina? That's why he asked you to dye your hair. He wanted you to look like her. Whenever you visited him, whenever he looked at a photo of you in your red lingerie, he pretended you were her."

Farrentina's gaze flicked over Risa, finally resting on her hair. Her eyes flashed with an edge of panic. "No. He loves me. Dryden loves *me*."

Trent leaned toward her. "Kane merely used you as a stand-in. A stand-in for Risa."

Farrentina shook her head adamantly, her hair whipping her cheeks. Her eyes glimmered with tears.

Trent pressed on. "He was at Risa's house this morning."

"No." Her breath came in short gasps. Her wide eyes snapped to the blackness beyond the window. "Damn police crawling all over the place. If they weren't here, he would have come to me." Tears broke free and streamed down her cheeks. "He would have come to *me*."

Risa closed her eyes. She didn't know what twisted road had led Farrentina to Kane, but she could bet it was a sad one, littered with abuse and neglect.

The same lonely road Dixie had traveled.

Guilt and regret and sorrow pounded at the back of Risa's eyes. If only she could go back in time. Remake decisions. Defend her sister. Try harder to let

Dixie know how special she was. Maybe then Dixie's life would have turned out differently.

Maybe *then* she wouldn't be in Kane's deadly grasp.

Chapter Eight

Tension coiling in his muscles, Trent paced the length
of his hotel room and tried to ignore the hiss of the
shower behind the closed bathroom door. He'd reported his progress to Donatelli as soon as he and
Rees had returned. He'd been over and over the interviews with Duane Levens and Farrentina Hamilton.
And he'd thumbed through copies of the reports on
Dixie's car and Risa's house that had been delivered
to the hotel room. Tomorrow he would confront Wiley, follow up on the three guards Farrentina had paid
off and meet with Warden Hanson.

He ran a hand over his face and through his hair.
He had a killer on the loose, an unknown person helping that killer and a mind-boggling amount of work
to do. And he still couldn't manage to keep his
thoughts off the sounds coming from behind that
bathroom door.

He should have known better than to insist Rees
stay in his hotel room tonight. But every time he'd
convinced himself to call the front desk and get her

another room, thoughts of Kane's past "artwork" invaded his mind, and he couldn't bear the idea of her even one door away.

The hiss of the shower stopped. A rustle filtered through the paper-thin door, undoubtedly the curtain sliding open. The soft flap of a bath towel followed.

Picturing terry cloth moving over bare skin, Trent almost groaned out loud. Having her in his room all night—close enough to hear her breathing, smell her scent, see her hair fanned out over the pillow as she slept—was going to be sheer torture. But if he wanted to protect her, if he wanted any semblance of peace of mind, he had no other choice.

He grabbed a pillow and an extra blanket from the closet shelf and threw them into one of the armchairs. Not the choicest sleeping arrangement, but it would have to do. Sleeping in the same bed with Rees was *not* an option.

He had just placed his Glock 9mm and his cell phone on the table within easy reach of the armchair when another sound rose from behind the door. A soft mew followed by silence.

The sound of crying.

His gut wrenched. Before he could stop himself, he was standing at the bathroom door, hand raised to knock.

Another soft mew drifted through the barrier.

He stilled his fist in midair. What did he think he was going to do? Ride into the bathroom like a white knight? Gather her in his arms? Kiss her tears away?

He'd already established he was no hero. He couldn't take her hurt away. He wasn't the man to comfort her. He had only to remember what happened this morning in this very hotel room to know that. The sweet flavor of her lips. The heat of her naked skin pressed to his. The wounded look in her eyes when he finally regained his senses and brought himself under control.

He let his fist fall to his side. The only way he knew to comfort her was to take her in his arms. And once her body molded to his, he didn't know if he could stop himself again.

Even if he could, he would only end up hurting her more.

He leaned his forehead against the door frame and listened, soaking up her pain, her frustration. Letting it swirl around inside him and mix with his own.

Slowly the silence lengthened and her sobs grew farther apart. He forced himself to push away from the door and move to the other side of the room. A few long minutes later, the bathroom door opened and she padded into the room.

She peered at him with red-rimmed eyes. Her flannel nightshirt fell halfway down her slim thighs, its boxy cut making her look all the more fragile. Strands of dark hair stuck to her cheeks, still moist with tears.

His fingers itched to smooth her hair back from her delicate face, but he forced his hands to remain riveted to his sides. "Are you all right?"

Tears welled up. She opened her eyes wide, as if to keep drops from spilling down her cheeks.

He bit his tongue. What a damn fool thing to say. Of course she wasn't all right. And she wouldn't be all right. Not until he found Kane. Not until he brought Dixie back to her, safe and sound. Not until he cleared out of her life and let her heal. "I'm sorry, Rees."

She swallowed hard and wrapped her arms around herself as if she was cold. "Me, too. About everything. Us. Kane. Dixie. Farrentina."

"Farrentina?"

She nodded. Her chin trembled, but she didn't allow a single tear to fall. "She's so much like Dixie. So needy. So damaged by life." She padded to the bed and perched on its edge. Shivering, she held herself tighter. "I wonder if Farrentina had a big sister. A big sister who abandoned her like I abandoned Dixie. A sister who could have made a difference but didn't."

He ached to take her in his arms, to soothe her old guilt, guilt he'd heard a hundred times. Guilt Rees dredged up every time Dixie made a bad decision, every time she engaged in risky behavior. "You were only a kid, Rees."

"I was ten years old."

"A kid. And you were living in an intolerable situation. You had a chance to get away from that house. A chance to live with your natural father in a normal, healthy home, and you took it. It was self-preservation. You can't beat yourself up for that.''

"I should have known she would be all alone. God knows, our mother had totally opted out of life by then. And her father never even acknowledged he had a daughter. I knew what it was like in that house, what her life would be like if I left. But I got out anyway. I left her behind.'' She shook her head, a shiver claiming her body. ''Dixie had no one.''

"You can't blame yourself, Rees.''

"Why not? She blames me for leaving her, you know. She always has. She got involved with Kane to punish me. And once she opened that door, all he had to do was make her believe he loved her. She was so hungry for love. She was an easy mark for that monster.'' The shivers racked her so hard, her teeth chattered.

"It's not your fault, Rees. There's no way a ten-year-old child should be expected to fill the roles of mother and father. You know that as well as I do.''

"Maybe.''

"Definitely. If this had happened to someone besides yourself, you would be telling her exactly that.''

She looked down at her folded arms and shivered. "You're probably right. I just want to change what happened. I want to make everything right.''

Regret slashed through him like a sharp blade. She'd always wanted to make things right. First with her mother and sister, then with him. But some things couldn't be made right. And some people couldn't be saved. He'd learned that looking at bodies of women and children who never deserved the kind of horror they'd endured. Women and children whose lives he could never restore, never make right again. "Sometimes you can't fix things. Sometimes things can never be right again."

She peered up at him, eyes moist. But she didn't cry. And somewhere, beneath the tears, beneath the pain, he saw the glimmer of light in her eyes. A light that had gone out in his own eyes long ago. "I can't believe that, Trent. I can never let myself believe that."

He closed his eyes and pressed his lids with his fingertips. Of course she couldn't. Not Rees. That was what made her who she was.

Opening his eyes, he studied her. So vulnerable, so frail, yet underneath, strong as steel. Another shiver racked her body.

He reached around her and pulled back the blanket and sheet. Guiding her down to the bed, he tucked her feet under the covers and rested her head back on the pillow. Taking a fortifying breath, he crawled into bed beside her, pulling the blankets up over them both.

She needed him. And if that meant holding her until she slipped into blessed unconsciousness, until she forgot her pain and worry and fear for a few short hours, he would do it.

Rolling to her side, she snuggled back against him,

fitting into the curl of his body like the missing piece of a puzzle.

Pain sharp and hot pierced his chest and ripped its way downward to his groin. Pain he couldn't stem. Pain he deserved.

He closed his eyes and listened to the ragged rhythm of her breathing slowly even out. In and out. In and out. He imagined the peace of sleep softening the worry in her face, soothing the regrets torturing her mind.

If only she'd let past feelings between them lie. Let them stay in the ground and decompose until the passing of time took all the pain, all the agony from them. Until nothing was left but dust.

But she hadn't.

And moreover, he hadn't.

And now once again the brilliant light of who she was and how she made him feel pierced the darkness of reality. Beckoned him. Tempted him. Tortured him.

He wanted to feel that light. To capture it. But if he reached out to take what she offered, he would eventually defile and destroy that very thing that made her who she was.

And that was one line he'd never allow himself to cross.

RISA CLOSED HER EYES and soaked in the heat of Trent's body cupping hers. She had finally stopped trembling, but the regret and pain spinning through her mind and clenching her muscles hadn't abated. Far from it. If possible, it had grown worse.

Having Trent this close, touching her, holding her, only served as a reminder of all she'd lost. All she'd never find again.

She reached for her anger, her constant companion for the past two years, the armor she'd shielded herself with, the only thing that had seen her through the pain.

But the anger wasn't there.

Trent had looked so concerned when she'd stepped out of the bathroom, concerned for her. He'd listened to her pain as if absorbing it himself. He'd tucked her in and cuddled her and cared for her.

How could she be angry with him?

Especially since she knew that everything he'd done, from breaking off their engagement two years ago to refusing to make love with her this afternoon, he'd done out of a misguided attempt to protect her.

She drew a deep breath and tried to keep tears from swamping her once more. She couldn't be angry with Trent, and that thought filled her with dread. Because if she couldn't gird herself with anger, all she had left was a broken heart and no defenses.

THE BLEAT OF THE CELL PHONE pierced Trent's troubled dream like a rending scream. He lurched from the bed and lunged for his phone on the little table by the window. He groped the dark with splayed fingers until his hand closed over cold plastic.

In the middle of the big bed, Rees sat straight up, the whites of her eyes visible in the dark room.

He tried not to look at her, tried not to convey his alarm. Phone calls in the middle of the night were never good. And he had a horrible feeling this one would be worse than most. Taking a bracing breath, he flipped the phone open and lifted it to his ear. "Burnell."

"Trent? Donatelli. We have a body. A woman. I need you to meet me at the scene."

Dread stabbed him. His gaze found Rees's and latched on. "Who is she, Vince?" He held his breath, waiting for the answer.

"No ID on her yet. The body was just discovered. I got the call myself less than a minute ago."

"Where is she?"

"That's the interesting part. Here the local cops have been driving by every half hour all night, and he laid her out right there in plain sight. I don't know how the hell he got in and out of there without being spotted."

Alarm blared in Trent's ears. *"Where the hell is she?"*

"On the front porch of Risa Madsen's house."

Chapter Nine

Night pressed in on the shadowed interior of Trent's rental car like a suffocating pall. Risa gasped for breath. Her pulse throbbed in her ears.

Dixie.

Trent hadn't wanted to bring her with him. It had just about killed him to allow her to climb into the passenger seat, she knew. But she *had* to go. She had to see for herself. She had to *know*. And in the end, Trent couldn't let her out of his sight. So here she was, speeding past the darkened windows of familiar houses on her way to a crime scene. A murder scene.

Dixie.

Trent swung onto her street and slowed to a crawl. A haze of humidity hung in the air, pulsing with the red and blue light of a half-dozen police cars. A cruiser blocked off either end of the street. Trent brought the car to a halt and flashed his identification before the uniforms waved him through.

Yellow tape draped from pickets ringing the perimeter of Risa's property. The house's empty windows reflected the throbbing red and blue light, and bright spotlights illuminated the driveway, the sidewalk, the porch.

Dixie.

Risa couldn't see the body from the interior of the car, but she knew it was there. Detectives and crime-scene technicians hovered around the front steps and small porch. A camera flash exploded as a police photographer snapped crime-scene photos.

Trent brought the car to a halt and reached for the door handle. "Stay in the car. I'll be right back."

She heard the tone of his voice, but his words seemed to bounce off her, an unintelligible jumble of sounds.

"Did you hear me, Rees? Stay here. I'll come back and get you."

She managed a nod.

He stared at her a long time, as if trying to look into her mind, to understand what she was thinking, feel what she was feeling. Finally he reached toward her and brushed a strand of hair from her cheek with tender fingertips. "Hang in there, Rees. It might not be her."

"And if it is?" her voice croaked, foreign to her own ears.

"You'll make it through, Rees. You'll survive, I promise."

She'd survive. She'd survive while Dixie succumbed. Just like when they were children.

She slumped in her seat. She was thirty. Thirty

years old. And Dixie was twenty-three. But still nothing had changed.

"I'll come back for you." Trent swung the car door open and climbed out. Cool spring air rushed into the interior, the scents of spruce and lilac strong and sweet. The door slammed behind him.

For a moment Risa merely sat still, breath coming in tortured gasps. Her mind swirled with images of tangled hair and pale, dead eyes. Images of Kane's evil. The thought that Dixie had been victimized by that evil sent waves of panic crashing through her.

No matter what she told Trent, she couldn't stay in the car. Horrific or not, she had to see. She had to know if the dead woman was Dixie. She couldn't think, couldn't breathe until she knew.

She grasped the handle of her door, the metal cold and solid under her fingers. Gathering her strength, she shoved the door open. Her head pounded. A hum rose in her ears. Hefting herself from the car, she forced her legs to support her weight.

One step. Two steps. She teetered across her lawn toward the police lights, toward the front porch of her house. The grass dragged at her shoes. The scents of spring swamped her, sticky as sweet syrup in the humid air.

Three steps. Four. The hum grew louder in her head, drowning out the murmur of voices, drowning out the pounding of her heart. She walked on. Over the grass. Up the cement walk. Closer and closer to the gathering of people. Closer and closer to the front porch.

Closer and closer to death.

Dixie.

The cloying odor of raw flesh clogged her throat. The stench of death turned her stomach. Still she forged ahead. She had to see for herself. She had to *know.*

The hum blared in her head like mind-numbing static. Her heart felt as if it was about to burst, her lungs about to collapse. She took the final steps to the porch, nudging between the circle of cops and technicians. Shoving her way through.

''Rees.'' From out of nowhere, Trent lunged for her, grasping her arm, trying to pull her away.

Red glistened from the open chest of the sprawled woman. Her brown hair was tangled around her pale face. Her hollow eyes stared into Risa's soul.

Farrentina Hamilton.

Horror and relief swept through Risa in a powerful wave. Her knees buckled. Her stomach retched. Strong arms grabbed her, pulled her close and swept her away.

Away from the body. Away from the smell. Away from the death.

Trent. She clung to him, burying her face in his strong shoulder. Sobs shook her body in fits and spurts, like shock waves after an earthquake. Horror numbed her mind.

TRENT HELD REES tight against him even after her sobs had waned. He shouldn't have left her in the car alone. If he had gotten an officer to stay with her, she wouldn't have reached the porch. She wouldn't have seen Farrentina's body. She wouldn't have witnessed Kane's true evil.

He pressed his cheek to her hair and breathed in her scent. Over the top of her head he could see Donatelli directing evidence technicians. The FBI agent would be chomping at the bit to use anything at his disposal to bring Kane down now that he had a body on his hands. And Rees would be at the top of his list.

Trent would have to hold him off for as long as possible. And to do that, he needed to give him an alternative. He glanced at Wiley, walking the perimeter of the crime scene. He could start with Farrentina's comments about the detective.

"I have to go, Rees."

She nodded, but she didn't let go.

He forced himself to pull back from her and look into her eyes.

She peered up at him. "I'll be okay." Her voice was firm, but her dilated pupils and the deathly white pallor of her skin told a different story.

He pressed his lips to her cool forehead. As much as he hated to let her out of the circle of his arms, he had to. His embrace might have been comforting at the moment she saw Farrentina's body. But in the long-term, he couldn't comfort her. He could only bring her more pain. Only drag her more deeply into Kane's evil undertow.

The one thing he *could* do was his job. Find Kane. Find Dixie. And find someone who could *truly* protect Rees.

He shifted as if to move away from her, but his arms wouldn't let go of her softness and his body wouldn't abandon her warmth. "I'll get an officer to take you back to the hotel and stand guard outside your door."

She swallowed hard and nodded.

"It's hard to say when I'll get back. I want to study the evidence here and attend the autopsy. And then there's the warden and Wiley and the guards Farrentina bribed."

"So it will be a while."

"Yes."

She drew a deep breath, as if bracing herself.

The urge to whisk her away to a safe place and personally stand guard over her tore at him.

She met his eyes and set her chin. "Chief Rook wanted to ask me some questions about Dixie. Will you tell him to come to the hotel?"

"You need to rest, Rees. You need to recover."

"While Kane does to Dixie what he did to Farrentina? No. I have to do whatever I can to stop him. And so do you."

"All right," he said, a sigh escaping his lips. There was no use arguing. Rees would drive herself into the ground if it meant even a sliver of a chance Dixie would return home alive. And he couldn't blame her. He'd done the same for people he'd never met. "I'll tell him."

"Thanks." She managed a shaky smile, a smile that didn't fool Trent for a minute. "I'll be fine, Trent. Just find Dixie. Before Kane kills her, too."

He looked deep into her dark eyes and nodded. Gritting his teeth, he forced himself to let her go.

MOST PEOPLE WOULDN'T THINK of human mortality as having an odor, but Trent knew better. It hung in the autopsy room, raw as peeled flesh and thick as blood. It colored the air like a red cloud and soaked so deeply into clothing fibers, hair and skin that even scrubbing with harsh detergents wouldn't remove all the residue.

"Burnell?" Donatelli passed the deputy coroner without giving him a glance and headed for Trent. Like Trent, he was clothed head to foot in protective clothing to fend off the smell and whatever fluids might splatter or smear. "I need to talk to you."

Trent braced himself for what was coming. "Shoot."

"I want to set a trap for Kane. And I want to use Risa Madsen as bait."

Thunder rose in Trent's ears. He wanted to object. He wanted to list the reasons why Donatelli couldn't involve Rees. He wanted to tell him the trap wouldn't work. But he couldn't lie. "And you want me to advise?"

"Yes. I want to get on it right away. Provided she hasn't changed her mind."

Trent forced a nod. Donatelli didn't have to worry about Rees changing her mind. Nothing would keep her from doing everything she could to save Dixie. If anything could, he would have thought of it by now. And used it. "We'll work on it after the autopsy."

Donatelli nodded. Checking his watch, he turned to the deputy coroner. "Shall we?"

The deputy coroner, a man known unimaginatively as "Doc," rasped out a heavy smoker's cough. Bright lights reflected off his round, cherry-red cheeks and nose, making him look more like Santa Claus than a man who dissected dead bodies for a living. "Isn't Pete Wiley supposed to be here? Or is it just going to be you Federal folks today?"

Trepidation twitched along Trent's nerves. He hadn't had a chance to confront the detective. But as soon as he showed, Trent aimed to get some answers from him. "We'll start without Wiley."

Next to him, Donatelli nodded. "Let's get this over with."

"Will do." With the flourish of a well-rehearsed tradition, Doc punched the Play button on the boom box in the corner and unveiled Farrentina Hamilton's body. Strains of Duke Ellington spiraled through the room, the energetic jazz a strange backdrop to the gruesome scene spread before them. Like Kane's other victims, a deep knife slit ran from her breastbone to her pubic bone.

Anger popped and crackled to life inside Trent, sucking the oxygen from the room. Heavy gloom hung over him like thick smoke. The sight of Farrentina's body would haunt him, torment him, like all the others. The cruelty she'd endured. The degradation and pain she'd felt in her last moments. The evil that had stolen her life.

Damn Kane. Damn him to hell.

Trent took notes, as Doc prodded and measured and dictated to his assistant, who photographed and painstakingly documented every wound Farrentina suffered. Ligature marks circled her wrists and neck. Her hands, knees and the bottoms of her feet were scuffed and gashed, debris clinging to the wounds. Like with the others, Kane had let her loose in the forest and hunted her down. Only after he'd killed her had he transported her body to Rees's house and displayed her for the police to find.

He'd had a secluded place to stage his hunt. A secluded place like Farrentina's vast estate? Impossible. If Kane had tortured her and hunted her down on her own property, the deputies staking out her house surely would have heard her screams. And since he and Rees had seen Farrentina mere hours before she died, Kane's secluded spot couldn't be too far from either Farrentina's house or Rees's.

He examined the debris sticking to the blood on her feet, hands and knees. To the naked eye it looked like it could have come from any forest in southern Wisconsin. But detailed analysis just might narrow down the area. That, along with what they knew about the time frame in which the murder occurred, could give them a location. And Trent had a feeling that if they found that secluded location, they'd find Kane.

"Tell the lab we need an analysis done on this debris ASAP," Trent said to Doc.

"Will do."

Doc's assistant began collecting the debris while Doc continued his prodding. Once he'd put every last bit in an evidence bag, he left for the lab.

Pete Wiley strode into the room in the assistant's wake, still pulling his protective clothing on over a wrinkled white shirt.

Doc looked up from the body, a dramatic frown turning down the corners of his mouth. "Nice you could show up, Pete. You got me up at this god-awful hour, and you don't even have the decency to show up on time?"

"Sorry to leave you here alone with the famous-but-incompetent, Doc."

Trent let Wiley's jab at the FBI slide off his back. He focused on the detective, taking in the lines of tension ringing his mouth, the shadows creasing the skin under his eyes. "We need to talk, Wiley."

Wiley's gaze shot to meet Trent's. An unmistakable shift of wariness crossed his sharp features. "What's up?"

"You tell me." He skewered Wiley with a glare. "Why didn't you tell Donatelli or me that Farrentina

Hamilton was bribing prison guards on Kane's behalf?''

Wiley glowered. A look of contempt colored his eyes. ''What's wrong? You feebs couldn't figure it out on your own?''

''That's not the way things work, and you know it, Wiley. We're supposed to work together.''

''Work together, my ass.'' He scoffed. ''You exaggerated a sighting you knew was bogus so you could take over.''

Trent eyed Wiley. He'd known from the beginning the detective wasn't happy to lose control of the manhunt. Could the detective's secretiveness merely be resentment of the FBI? He had to admit it was possible. He'd seen it before. Many times. ''Care to explain how you stumbled upon the bribery in the first place, Detective?''

''Ever hear of police work? You should try it some time.''

''I want answers, Wiley.''

''One of the other guards tipped me off a few weeks ago. Complained that Kane was getting preferential treatment. Apparently he reported it to the warden, but he didn't get results. He thought Hanson might be sharing in some of the green flying around. I was investigating before Kane escaped.''

Trent nodded. Wiley's explanation sounded plausible. And it would be easy to check.

''I know what you're trying to do, Burnell. You're trying to find the man who helped Kane so you can keep your little professor from putting herself on a hook. Well, don't bother looking at me. Whether I've let you in on it or not, I've done my job. I've turned the lives of those three guards upside down and haven't found a damn thing beyond them trading TV time for a little cash.''

Donatelli straightened. ''You'd damn well better get me copies of those reports, Detective.''

''Turned 'em over to one of your men on my way here.''

Trent's mind raced. The guards weren't the only ones in position to help Kane escape. There was still Warden Hanson. As if reading his thoughts, Wiley grinned knowingly. ''If you're betting on the warden giving you some answers, don't. I've been through his financial records. His wife's aunt died recently and gave him an infusion of cash. Other than that, the man lives within his means. Besides, we've had officers watching him and his wife since you alerted us last night. So far he's gone to work, and she shopped for handbags. Not exactly suspicious activities.''

Maybe not. But a few hours of working and shopping didn't let Warden Hanson off the hook. He had a powerful motive to help Kane. Motive that had nothing to do with money, and everything to do with revenge.

Trent narrowed his eyes on the detective. Hanson wasn't the only possibility. Wiley himself was guilty of plenty of suspicious activity. ''You obviously dislike Risa Madsen. And her sister. Why?''

"What does it matter? I haven't let it compromise the case. I've done my job. By the book."

That was well and good. But it didn't answer the question. "What do you have against them?"

"What the hell *don't* I have against them, that's what you should be asking." He shook his head, his mouth twisting into a sneer. "Do you want to know what I think about women like them? Do you really want to know?"

Trent said nothing, just waited for him to continue.

"Women who find monsters like Kane titillating? Women who find toying with that kind of danger fun? Whether they are marrying him or studying him, it's all the same. They're equally sickening. If he got the chance, he'd string 'em up and torture and kill them in a minute. Look at Ms. Hamilton here."

Trent followed his gaze to the ravaged body in front of them. He didn't bother to point out the differences between Rees studying the criminally deviant and Dixie and Farrentina's obsession with Kane. Wiley was obviously deaf to logic on that issue.

"They don't want to see what a monster he really is. They'd rather see him as fascinating, exciting, even a victim of big bad law enforcement. They blame us and glorify him. It makes me sick."

Though Wiley's derision of Rees and lack of understanding for Dixie and Farrentina rubbed Trent the wrong way, he could understand the detective's frustration. He'd felt it himself more than once. But where did that leave him? Wiley might be guilty of many things, but helping Kane wasn't among them.

"Fellas, before you do much more talking, I think you'll want to take a look at this."

Trent tensed at the urgency in Doc's voice. Deep in the chest cavity, something glinted dully in the bright lights. Something metal.

After snapping a series of photos, Doc reached into the cavity with a forceps and grasped the object. A silver chain, muted by blood, unfurled as he pulled. A silver locket emerged on the end of the chain. Doc held up the find.

Donatelli leaned forward, trying to get a better look. "A locket? What the hell is that doing inside her?"

Trent's stomach hardened like a cold, tight fist. He thought of the photo of Rees and Dixie with the teddy bears. In that photo, Dixie had worn a locket. A locket that looked very much like this one. "Open it."

Doc grasped the locket gingerly with latex-gloved fingers and pressed the release. The tiny door flipped open.

Folded inside was a photo of Rees posing on the front steps of her house—the steps where Kane had displayed Farrentina's body. The photo was slit down the middle, just as the photo of Dixie had been. And at the bottom of the photo a single word had been finely etched in blood.

Mine.

Dread tightened around his throat like strong fingers. He stepped away from the body, pulse hammering in his ears, drowning out the beat of Doc's jazz.

He'd finish with Wiley later. He'd go over the autopsy protocols later. Now he had to get to Rees.

He only prayed to God he wasn't too late.

RISA PACED ACROSS the hotel room and looked at her watch for the tenth time in the past ten minutes. Rook had said he'd be over as soon as he was finished at the crime scene. He'd said the questions he needed to ask were important—urgent—and that she should stay at the hotel until he arrived.

He should have been here by now.

A myriad of explanations for his tardiness pingponged through her mind. Had the police found a lead? Had they found Kane himself?

Or had they found another body? A body they wouldn't dare tell her about over the phone? *Dixie's body.*

She looked at the telephone. She couldn't even call Trent and ask. It had been difficult for him to leave her alone. And as much as she wanted his arms around her, as much as she wanted him to make her feel safe and strong, she couldn't call him now. She certainly didn't want her worry to send him racing back to her side when he needed to spend his time and energy guiding the search for Kane.

She thought of the uniformed officer standing outside the door. Deputy Perry had a two-way radio. He might know what was going on. She strode to the door.

When she pulled it open, Perry's friendly blue eyes snapped to her. His doughy face flattened in a grin. "What can I do you for, Professor?"

Faced with his confident but relaxed manner, Risa flushed. She was probably just being paranoid. But paranoid or not, she had to know. "Chief Rook should be here by now. Have you heard if anything urgent is going on? Anything that would detain him?"

The officer shook his head and rested a hand on his radio. "Not a thing. I'll let you know if any news comes through."

She offered him a grateful smile. "Thanks. I appreciate it."

"Anything else?"

"No, I'm fine." As fine as she could possibly be in such a situation.

"If you want something to eat, you can go ahead and order room service." He gave her an encouraging nod, and she had to wonder if he was really concerned about filling her stomach, or filling his own.

Though she hadn't eaten anything but a vending machine sandwich since she'd heard of Kane's escape, she couldn't even think of food without sending her stomach into somersaults. "No, I'm fine. Would you like me to order you something?"

Perry shook his head. "No ma'am. I was just concerned about you. You've been through a lot lately from what I understand.''

She gave him a warm smile and started to close the door. ''Thanks, Deputy.''

''Make sure you refasten that dead bolt.''

She closed the door and slid the dead bolt home. And then she fastened the chain lock, too.

Nerves edgy as before, she resumed her pacing, glancing at her watch once more, just in time to see another minute tick past.

She was exhausted. She'd slept for a couple of hours last night. But that had been with Trent's arms around her. Protecting her. Infusing her with strength. Now, with the light of morning peeking around the edges of the drapes and the events of the past few hours playing endlessly in her mind, there wasn't a chance she could shut her eyes. And sleep? It was a distant, unreachable fantasy.

The doorknob rattled, followed by a knock.

Risa's heart jumped in her chest. Had Rook finally arrived? Or had Deputy Perry heard something on his radio? She scurried across the room and reached for the doorknob. A shiver skittered along her nerves, stopping her short.

Standing on her tiptoes, she peered through the peephole and out into the hallway.

Cold, dead eyes set in a boyish face stared back at her from the other side of the door. Hatred reached through the peephole and clutched her throat, tightening until she couldn't breathe.

Dryden Kane.

He smiled, lips pulling back from straight, white teeth. A loud scrape echoed through Risa's paralyzed mind. A knife blade biting into wood.

Chapter Ten

Pulse thrumming in his head, Trent drove as fast as safety would allow. He had to get to Rees. He couldn't be too late.

He'd called the sheriff's department and local police as soon as he'd stepped from the autopsy room. They should reach the hotel before he did. He could only pray they reached the hotel before Kane as well.

Taking the last corner without slowing, he whipped the car into the hotel's parking lot and drove straight for the entrance. Sun sparked off the cop cars barring the entrance and flanking the building. Blue and red lights flashed like flickering sparks of fire. Even before he stomped the brake pedal, he spotted the uniforms at the wide glass doors, stopping hotel residents from entering. Or leaving.

Securing a crime scene.

Breath jammed in his throat. He threw the car into park, opened the door and scrambled out. Identification in hand, he raced up the shallow steps. He flashed his ID and surged inside.

Voices jangled through the lobby. Deputies corralled guests and cut off possible escape routes.

Trent glanced toward the elevators. The doors gaped open, incapacitated. He rushed for the stairs, flashing his ID again before he plunged into the stairwell. He took the steps two at a time. Fear pulsed inside him, living and raw. He had to find Risa. She had to be all right.

Reaching the third floor, he pushed the door open with shaking hands. The smell of death smeared the air. Stepping into the hall, his heart lurched.

Blood pooled around a blue-uniformed body. A flat, friendly face stared up at him, frozen in horror, blue eyes fixed in death.

Deputy Perry.

The sight hit Trent like a kick to the gut. Kane had slit Perry's throat. Slit his throat, so he could get to Rees.

Heart clutching, Trent circled the body and lunged through the hotel room's open door.

Rees huddled in the corner chair, her arms wrapped protectively around herself. Her cheeks were void of color, and she was trembling so hard he could see it from across the room.

Grantsville's young police chief hovered over her, pen and pad in hand.

Trent crossed the room in four strides. Bulldozing Rook out of the way, he fell to his knees and engulfed her in his arms.

A breath of relief tore from his lips. He buried his

face in her hair, its soft lavender scent chasing away the odor of death. Kane hadn't gotten to her. At least not physically. She was here and whole.

And scared to death.

Fury slashed through him in a wave of fire. Damn Kane. The killer must have been watching her house, enjoying the rush of police to the scene he'd caused. Watching their horrified reaction to his "artwork." Soaking in the power he held over others. He must have spotted Risa at the scene and followed her back to the hotel.

Trent should have known Kane would want to see his audience. He should have suspected the serial killer would lurk nearby, watching the flashing lights. He should have known that bringing Rees to the scene would put her in jeopardy. He should have known because *he knew Kane.* He'd lived in the killer's mind. He'd walked in the killer's shoes. He'd dreamed the killer's dreams for two long years.

So why had he taken Rees with him? Why hadn't he left her stashed in the hotel? And once he had placed her squarely in Kane's path, why in the hell had he let her out of his sight, sending her back to the hotel with only one deputy to protect her?

He could have lost her. Lost her forever.

Panic gripped his chest and squeezed. He struggled to keep calm, to breathe.

He hadn't thought Kane would come for Rees this quickly. He'd thought he would kill other women first, biding his time as he'd done with his first wife. But he'd been wrong. Dead wrong.

He hadn't lost Rees. She was here in his arms. No thanks to him. Forcing himself to let her go, he pulled back and looked in her glazed eyes. "What happened?"

"He tried to get in, but Deputy Perry told me to lock—" She covered her mouth with trembling fingers. "I looked through the peephole. He just smiled at me. And his eyes. His cold, dead eyes..."

Another wave of rage whipped through Trent. He struggled to hold on to his composure. He couldn't give in to his anger with Kane. His anger with himself. Not now. Rees needed him now. He had to stay calm for her. He rubbed his hands up and down her arms, trying to warm her, as if a simple chill was responsible for her trembling. "Go on."

"He cut the door from top to bottom with his knife and looked through the peephole as though he could see me. As though he was cutting *me*." A shudder shook her body.

Trent ground his teeth together. What he wouldn't give to have Kane here right now. What he wouldn't give to beat the SOB to bloody death with his bare fists.

Rees drew in a shaky breath. "And then he just walked away. I called 911. It wasn't until Chief Rook got here that I knew what Kane had done to Deputy Perry." She bit her bottom lip. Tears broke free and slipped silently down her cheeks. She closed her eyes, long lashes brushing smooth cheeks. A strand of chocolate hair drifted against pale skin.

Trent raised his hand to her face and brushed the strand from her cheek. His fingers skimmed the satin of her hair, the silk of her skin.

What would he have done if Kane had gotten to her?

He didn't know. And thank God he didn't have to find out. She was safe. At least for now.

At least until he put her in Kane's path again. And that time would come soon. Except this time, he would be placing her in front of Kane on purpose.

The thought hit him with such force, it knocked the breath from his lungs. He gasped for air. In the autopsy room, Donatelli had brought up setting the trap for Kane. Trent had known it was inevitable, but he hadn't really faced it. He'd pushed the prospect from his mind in favor of other more pressing things. Other less painful options. But with Kane's current body count up to two—the second a deputy—he couldn't deny it any longer. He had to face it. They would set a trap. As soon as possible.

And Rees would be the bait.

Wrapping his arms around her, he pulled her against him. He soaked in the feel of her, the scent of her. He had to tell her. And although he knew damn well she wanted just this—to lure Kane, to do whatever she could to save Dixie—using her to bait a trap would be one of the hardest things he'd ever done. It wasn't her reaction to the plan that bothered him. It was his own.

He nestled his lips in the shell of her ear and took one last breath of her sweet scent. "We have to talk." Despite his attempt to stay calm, a note of fear and anger rang in his voice, loud as a cymbal crash in the hushed room.

She pulled back from his arms and searched his eyes. Her face blanched bone-white. "What happened, Trent?"

"It's not what has happened. It's what is going to happen." He glanced at Rook, still hovering over them. Although the police chief would likely know every detail of the plan in a few hours, the last thing Trent needed was an audience to witness the anguish burning inside him like corrosive acid.

He glanced around the hotel room. Blood spatter stained the scarred door gaping open to the hall beyond. He couldn't take Rees out that door. Not until Perry's body had been taken away.

Audience or not, he had to tell her.

"What's going on, Trent?" Her worried gaze clung to his.

He took a deep breath and pushed the words past his lips. "We're setting a trap for Kane."

She nodded and her mouth flattened into a line. "And you're going to use me to lure him?"

"Yes."

"Good." Her gaze traveled over his face, finally coming to rest on his eyes. Her pupils were dilated, her eyes moist. But despite the glimmer of tears, despite the shock she'd been through, that inner glow shone from their depths, clear and unshakable as ever. She laid her hand on his arm. "You're right to do this, you know. It's the only thing you can do."

"Yes." The word lodged in his throat. God, he prayed he was doing the right thing. He prayed he wasn't merely placing Rees right where Kane wanted her. Because the stakes were far too high to be wrong now.

RISA SLIPPED INTO the chair next to Trent in the Grantsville police station's conference room. In one short day, the place had been transformed into a war room with maps and pictures and diagrams lining the walls. A dozen FBI agents and sheriff's deputies jammed around the conference table, the low hum of voices constant as the drone of bees. The odors of stale coffee and stress soured the air.

At the head of the room, Vince Donatelli stood in front of a large map of southwestern Wisconsin. Colored pins and circles stabbed and stretched over several counties. He pointed to a vast area stretching from Grantsville nearly to Madison. "According to the last time Farrentina Hamilton was seen alive at her house, the approximate time of her death and the time her body was discovered at Professor Madsen's house, the victim had to have been murdered somewhere in this vicinity."

Risa studied the circle plotted on the map. Much

of the area was in the unglaciated region of Wisconsin, a land of steep hills, deep gorges and dotted with a few tiny towns and family farms in the southwest corner of the state. Sparsely populated land where Kane could stage his hunt and no one would hear his victim's screams.

"The debris found on the victim's body is consistent with this area as well," Donatelli continued.

The victim's body. The image of Farrentina in death crashed through her mind once again, followed by Deputy Perry's soft, flat face. An involuntary shiver shot up her spine.

She balled her fists under the table and shoved the disturbing images from her mind. Kane wouldn't claim another victim. Not if she could help it. That was why she was attending this briefing. That was why she was putting her life on the line. To save Dixie. And to prevent Kane from killing anyone else.

Vince Donatelli glanced down at one of the reports littering the table in front of him. "We know he has some sort of car or truck, but reports of stolen vehicles haven't yielded results as of yet."

Risa felt Trent shift in the chair next to her, but she didn't glance his way. She didn't want to see the worry in his eyes, the tension in his every muscle. She knew his decision to go along with setting the trap for Kane had been a hard one to make. Including her went against every protective instinct he had nurtured over the years. He wanted to set her aside where she would be safe. Distant, but safe. Only the prospect of Kane killing more people had convinced him to use her to bait his trap for Kane.

Donatelli tapped the map with a finger. "We have roadblocks set on these highways, checking all vehicles leaving the vicinity. Sheriff's departments from these counties are combing the area with helicopters and dogs."

"It'll take days to cover that much ground. Even with helicopters," Wiley piped up from the back of the room. "I doubt we have that much time before he kills again."

Donatelli shook his head. "That's where Professor Madsen comes in."

All eyes in the room settled on Risa. She straightened in her chair. She knew the general idea of the trap they would set. Trent had given her some hints of what he was thinking. So she could prepare: pack her clothing, call the university to cover her classes. But she had yet to hear the details.

Donatelli's eyes rested on Trent. "Burnell?"

Following the path of Donatelli's gaze, she drew in a breath of sour air and held it.

Trent looked up at the sound of his name as if he'd just snapped awake after a nightmare-plagued nap. Lines dug into his forehead and flanked his eyes and mouth. His eyes seemed more intense against the pale of his skin.

A tremor unfurled in her rib cage, right under her heart. She pulled her eyes from his and focused on the map.

Trent glanced around the room at the FBI agents and deputies who would be setting the trap. "Kane will come after Professor Madsen again. But this time we can use his aggressiveness to our advantage." Trent's baritone rumbled like an approaching thunderstorm.

The tremor worked its way through Risa's chest and into her arms and legs. She gripped her thighs under the table to keep her hands from shaking.

Trent turned, his steel gaze drilling into her. "We are going to set you up in a bed-and-breakfast just north of Grantsville. We've evacuated the couple who owns the place." His voice lowered in an intense yet intimate rumble, as if the details of the trap were a secret just between the two of them.

She forced herself to concentrate on his words, on the details of the trap. Not on his voice. Not on the warmth it inspired deep inside her.

And not on the fear tightening her nerves.

"We'll set up a patrol so Kane will believe we're watching over you." He glanced up, his gaze scanning the agents in the room as if trying to pick out the very best ones for the job. "The more challenging the setup, the better. Kane's bold, and he likes thumbing his nose at authority. It makes him feel powerful. Invincible."

She thought of Kane's cold eyes peering through the peephole in the hotel room door. His cocky smile as the knife's blade bit into wood. Under the table, she dug her fingernails into her palms.

"I suspect he's either watching Professor Madsen's house, watching this police station, or getting his information through a leak. So we'll stop by the house and pack some clothes, and we'll leak her location. And when Kane shows up—and he will—we'll have plenty of agents and local police within striking distance."

The walls inched a little closer. There wasn't enough air in the room. Risa had never suffered an anxiety attack before, but she knew the signs. She closed her eyes and scooped air into her lungs. She had reason to be anxious. The worry in Trent's eyes told her that much. But fear wasn't going to keep her from doing whatever she could for Dixie. Not when her sister's life depended on her. Not when other lives depended on her.

As if sensing her need for support, Trent rested his hand on her arm. "You won't be alone, Rees. An agent will be staying with you at all times."

She shook her head, the steady, frantic pulse rising in her ears. She hadn't been alone when Kane had come for her in the hotel. Deputy Perry had been assigned to protect her. But it hadn't mattered. Kane had still gotten within a few feet of her. But that's not what bothered her. Far from it. What bothered her was the image of Deputy Perry's flat face flecked with blood. His twinkling eyes staring in death.

She couldn't let Trent assign an agent to watch over her only to set that agent up as a sitting duck. She couldn't be responsible for the loss of another

life, even if the risk was part of the agent's job. She
glanced around the room, at all the eyes watching,
waiting for the rest of the plan to be laid on the table.
"I need to talk to you, Trent."

Trent raised a questioning brow.

She pushed her chair back and stood. "Please."

Sensing her desperation, he nodded and pushed his
own chair back from the table. Rising to his feet, he
followed her into the hall.

Once the door closed behind them and the quiet of
the empty hall enveloped them, Risa whirled to face
him. "Let me stay in the house alone."

Trent narrowed his eyes and shook his head. "Absolutely not."

"I keep thinking of Officer Perry. He was such a
nice man. He was so concerned about me. And now
he's dead. He gave his life to protect me." She
splayed her hands in front of her. She had to make
him see. She had to make him understand. "And now
you want to assign someone to watch over me again,
someone who might be killed. You can't do that."

"I'll be the agent with you, Rees."

Alarm shook her to her toes. "No."

"You don't expect me to dangle you in front of
Kane's nose and not be there with you, do you?"

Of course not. Why hadn't she seen it before? Trent
would insist on being there. He'd insist on protecting
her. It would be the only way he could go along with
setting the trap.

Cold fear swept over her. She'd been worried sick

about a stranger laying his life on the line for her. But this was even worse. She couldn't bear the thought of Trent in danger, Trent putting himself in Kane's path. "No, Trent. Please."

He narrowed his eyes on her, his steel gaze piercing, probing. "So you don't believe what you said."

She gave him a questioning look.

"Don't you remember? In the hotel room yesterday you said we are stronger together than we are apart. You don't really believe that, do you?"

She drew in a sharp breath. Her own words echoed in her ears. *I was stronger in your arms just now than I am alone. We were stronger.*

She'd said those words, and she'd meant them. But could she still stand by them now? Now that being together included a risk to Trent's life?

She gnawed the inside of her bottom lip. She wanted to protect Trent. She wanted to keep him far away from the house, far away from Kane. She wanted to keep him out of the path of evil and danger.

Wasn't that what Trent had been trying to do with her all along? Wasn't the choice he made two years ago when he broke off their engagement the same choice she was considering now?

She swallowed hard. It was the same. With one difference. *She* couldn't make that choice. She couldn't push him away, no matter how much she wanted to. Because even if *he* didn't believe they were stronger together, *she* did. And she had to stick by her words, stick by her belief. She couldn't do things any other way. "We are stronger together, Trent. I believe it with my whole heart."

He nodded, as if he'd known the answer all along. As if he'd counted on it. His steel-gray eyes drilled into her soul. "Then prove it."

Chapter Eleven

Oak limbs thick and dense with leaves arched over the car, shadowing the drive from the moon's light. Trent piloted around the curves in silence, his eyes glued to the road in front of him, his mind on the woman beside him.

Using Rees's words against her had been a dirty trick, but he'd do it again in a heartbeat if it meant convincing her to go along with his plan. There wasn't a chance in hell he would let her face Kane alone.

He allowed his gaze to skate over her for a moment. Her ramrod-straight back. The way she folded her arms over her chest as if shielding her tender heart. She hadn't said more than two words since they'd climbed in his car. And neither had he. There was nothing to say but silent prayers. Nothing to do but wait.

He breathed in her lavender scent, but it did nothing to loosen the tension that wound around his nerves as tight as a hangman's noose. It only added another layer of tension. A layer he'd tried to forget over the past two years, a layer he couldn't afford to think about now.

If only he could turn the car around. If only he could whisk Rees far away from Kane and FBI traps and danger. If only he could leave all of it behind.

They could get lost. Someplace where neither Kane nor the FBI could ever find them. He and Rees could buy a house and raise a family and be happy—like they'd always planned. Like they'd always dreamed.

But that was impossible.

Even if they could get away, even if they could buy a little house and raise a family, he could never turn his back on the people who needed him—the victims and their families. He could never forget the death and depravity. He'd been right to give up those dreams two years ago. And no matter how much he wished his life was different, he could never go back. He should know that by now. He should accept it.

But somehow, in the warmth of her presence, he wanted to forget everything—Kane, Dixie, the FBI's trap. He wanted to take Rees into his arms and hold on for dear life.

He wanted to be purely selfish.

The thick canopy of leaves and limbs opened into a clearing, and moonlight spilled from the sky. Set like a jewel in the center of a wide lawn stood an elegant Victorian bed-and-breakfast. Its round turret reached heavenward. Gingerbread flanked the eaves.

And on the front porch, a bench swing swayed back and forth in the light breeze. The Lilac Inn.

He stopped the car.

"It's beautiful," Rees breathed beside him.

"Yes." It was beautiful. And romantic. But tonight the romance of the setting was strung with a tense thread of danger.

"It reminds me of that place on Chesapeake Bay." Her voice deepened and caught. "The place we were going to spend our honeymoon."

He remembered. Too well. He'd made the reservations before he'd left for Wisconsin. Before he'd joined the investigation into the deaths of the five college coeds. Before Kane had slithered his way into Trent's mind and stained his soul.

When he'd returned, he'd canceled the reservation. Canceled his wedding. Canceled his future.

He forced his mind to focus on the scene in front of him. A wide, well-groomed lawn stretched out from the house on all sides before blending into acre after acre of state park forest. Forest that offered seclusion so no innocent bystanders would be hurt.

The setup was perfect.

Next to him, Rees shivered and followed his gaze to the black outline of forest looming on the edge of the lawn and folded her arms tighter over her chest. "Do you think Kane is out there right now?"

"Not tonight. He's not stupid. He knows we have plenty of agents and deputies stationed throughout the woods. He'll wait until we relax our guard. Until he thinks we don't expect him.''

She nodded, but she didn't take her eyes from the blackness outside the window. Her mouth tightened as if she was biting the inside of her bottom lip to cease its trembling. As she always did when trying to hide her emotions.

He longed to enfold her in his arms. To kiss away the tension. To be her strength and let her be his.

A longing he could never satisfy.

KNEES QUAKING, Risa stood in the doorway and glanced around one of the Lilac Inn's intimate guest rooms. White tulle draped and frothed over the canopy bed like a wedding veil. The fragrance of eucalyptus and fresh-cut lilacs laced the air. And through the open bathroom door, she could see candles surrounding a claw-footed bathtub, deep and big enough for two.

The FBI might as well have put her up in a stone dungeon complete with torture chamber. She'd have preferred that to being shut in this romantic fantasy with Trent, waiting for Kane to appear at any moment and end all her illusions. All her hopes.

She forced her feet to cross to the window. Pulling the lace curtains aside with trembling hands, she peered through rippled glass at the row of lanterns sparkling along the driveway.

A shadowed figure strode toward the house, an obviously heavy box in hand. She'd recognize Trent's silhouette anywhere, the sharp turn of his head as he surveyed the forest, the broad framework of his shoulders. But tonight his normally fluid stride was tight, abrupt. His broad shoulders were slumped as if protecting a wound. Trent was in pain. She could see it as clearly as if he were cut and bleeding.

An answering ache throbbed deep inside her.

The past days had been one horror piled on top of another. Dixie's kidnapping. Kane's threats. Farrentina and Deputy Perry's murders. And now the worry of Trent risking his life alongside her. But even with all that had happened, even with fear and evil hovering over her like a shroud, she could still hold on to the hope that Kane would be caught and Dixie returned safely. And she knew sooner or later the nightmare would end, and the sun would come up in the morning and chase away the darkness.

Trent had none of those assurances.

When this case was over, he would go on to the next gruesome serial murder. And the next. He would immerse himself in other killers' evils, in other victims' fears. The darkness would never let up for him. The nightmare would never end.

And the worst of it was, he would travel his dark path alone.

A shiver claimed her. She rubbed her upper arms in a futile attempt to chase away the chill. She could only imagine what his life had been like the two years since Dryden Kane's evil had first touched him, the two years since he'd pushed her away. Day after day of being confronted with unspeakable horrors. Night after night of loneliness. Darkness.

And that's the life he would return to. Unless she could make him see he didn't have to be alone. Unless she could make him believe they were better together. Stronger.

Letting the lace curtain fall, she turned her back on the window. It was no use. He hadn't allowed himself to believe two years ago. And she had even less reason to think he would allow himself to believe now. But she couldn't leave him alone in his dark world. She wouldn't. And if there was a way to lift some of the darkness from his life, even if it was only for a brief period of time, she would find it.

At least she had to try.

The slam of the front door and thunk of his footsteps climbing the staircase cut into her thoughts. Drawing a deep breath, she turned from the lace and candles and strode out the door into the seating area at the head of the stairs.

Trent set the heavy file box he'd been carrying on the coffee table in front of a damask love seat. Straightening, he turned to face her and clawed a hand through his hair. "How are you holding up?"

"I'm fine." She forced a casualness into her voice she didn't feel. "The rooms are beautiful."

"Yes, they are." The glow of a hurricane lamp highlighted the hard planes of his face, sinking his eyes in shadow. Tension stiffened his shoulders and back, obvious even under his rumpled white shirt. "I have some sandwiches downstairs if you're hungry."

Her throat was too dry to swallow, and her stomach too tense to even think about digesting. "Thanks, but I'm not."

"Thirsty? There's lemonade."

"No, thanks." She looked down at the box on the coffee table behind him. "Kane's files?"

His head bobbed in a tense nod. "I thought I'd go through them again. See if there's anything I'm missing. Anything that would point to who helped Kane or where he might be."

She frowned at his pointed use of the word *I*. No doubt he planned to burn the midnight oil poring over files while she was safely tucked in bed. "I want to help."

"These are FBI files, Rees."

She knew very well what they were. And she knew the real reason he didn't want her to help him go through them had only partially to do with keeping FBI files confidential and everything to do with protecting her from the horrible images captured in the crime-scene photos.

She also knew arguing about it would get her nowhere. Besides, she didn't want to argue. "What has your life been like the past two years, Trent?"

A furrow dug between his brows. He narrowed his eyes as if trying to figure out where the question had come from and where it might lead. "What do you mean, what has it been like?"

"What do you do? In a normal day? In a normal week?"

The furrow deepened. "I work a lot."

That much was obvious. And if Trent used the words "a lot," she'd be willing to bet he worked nearly every waking hour. And that he didn't sleep much. "Is that all you do? Work?"

"I go to the gym."

The gym, of course. Exercising had always been Trent's way of trying to cope with stress. And from the well-sculpted biceps evident under his wrinkled sleeves, he had been trying to cope with more than his share over the past two years.

"Do you do anything else? Anything besides working and going to the gym?"

"There's no time for anything else." He turned his back on her and resumed shuffling through the files.

Just as she'd suspected. A life filled with nothing but darkness. No wonder he felt he was tainted, that he'd contaminate anything he touched. She circled the love seat and stepped toward him, cornering him between the love seat and the coffee table. "Why don't you make time for something else?"

He blew a frustrated breath through tight lips. "Make time for what, Rees? Needlepoint?"

She let his sarcasm slide off her back. "For something other than death and murder and darkness. For something good in your life. Something uplifting."

His frown turned to a glower. "What is your point?"

"My point? My point is that you've let Kane take over your life."

"He's escaped from prison. He kidnapped your sister. He has killed two people so far, and he's after you. Of course he has taken over my life."

She held up a hand. She wasn't going to let him obscure the bigger picture. "Not just since he escaped. But every day for the past two years. You've let him get under your skin. You've let him cut everything good out of your life. Everything except darkness and evil and death."

"Evil and darkness and death is my job, Rees. What would you have me do? Quit?" He scowled and shook his head, as if the idea was as despicable as some of the men he tracked down. "If I walk away, more people die."

"I'm not suggesting you walk away. I would never suggest that."

"Then what *are* you suggesting?"

She bit the inside of her lip, trying to still its trembling, the trembling that claimed every nerve, every muscle. She wanted to suggest that he love her, that he marry her, that they resume the life they had planned together, a life filled with children and joy, a life Kane destroyed. But that would be a waste of breath. "Talk to me. Here. Now. Maybe I can help." Holding her breath, she watched his eyes. She waited for his answer.

His scowl faded and the hard planes of his face softened. "You can't help."

"But I know Kane. And I know you. I may be the only one who can help."

"You can't help, Rees."

She narrowed her eyes, studying the concern lining his forehead, the tension clenching his neck and shoulders. "You still believe you'll contaminate me, don't you?"

A muscle flexed along his jaw, but he said nothing. A silence as telling as if he'd shouted "yes" at the top of his voice.

"It's not you who is tainted, Trent. It's the criminals you profile. Your career as a profiler is only *part* of who you are."

Releasing a breath, he shook his head. "It's not something you can separate. This job changes a person, Rees. It makes you look at the world in an entirely different way. It *becomes* who you are." He searched her face, his eyes imploring her to understand.

"I understand what you're saying Trent, but—"

"No, you don't. And I'm doing a damn poor job of explaining." He pinched the bridge of his nose as if the pressure would help him come up with a way to make her see where he was coming from. His mouth flattened into a grim line. Dropping his hand, he looked at her. Sadness and regret ached in his eyes. "I'll bet your stomach is tied in a big damn knot. That's why you aren't interested in those sandwiches downstairs, even though you've eaten only once in the past forty-eight hours."

Judging from the look on Trent's face, he didn't need an answer. She bit her tongue and let him go on.

"And sleep? You've gotten about three hours since I first knocked on your door."

Another statement she couldn't refute.

"You can't eat. You can't sleep. Kane has destroyed your piece of mind, Rees. And it can't be fixed. You'll never feel safe again. Even if this trap works like a charm. Even if we get Dixie back. Even if we catch Kane. You'll never walk up the front steps of your house without seeing Farrentina Hamilton's body. You'll never look through a peephole without seeing Kane's eyes staring back at you."

Risa flinched at his words. He was right. Those events would haunt her the rest of her life. Even now she couldn't imagine returning to her little bungalow. She couldn't imagine sleeping inside those walls again.

"And the longer you are exposed to Kane's brand of evil, the worse it gets. Believe me. It eats at you until every man you see looks like a killer. Until every stranger's smile seems like a threat." He closed his eyes and scrubbed his face with his fingers, as if trying to erase images only he could see. Images of brutality and death and evil that were now seared into his mind permanently.

Drawing a deep breath, he opened his eyes and looked into hers. "And then nothing in the world is carefree anymore. Nothing is wholesome. Nothing is safe. From the moment you wake to the time you finally close your eyes—if you can—all you can recognize is evil and danger and death.''

An involuntary shiver claimed her.

He reached out and ran his hand down her arm, as if trying to warm the chill inside her. A chill that could only be chased away by his embrace. ''Take those feelings and multiply them by hundreds of cases a year. That's what it is like for me. You talk about evil and darkness and death. I know them intimately. They're inside me. Part of me. I can't separate them.''

She reached out and grasped his arm as if to support him. As if she could do something to stem the flow of pain.

''While working on Kane's case two years ago, I realized I'd crossed the line. I seemed to have lost the ability to see anything through normal eyes. I couldn't enjoy anything, not a sunny day. Not a warm breeze. Not the scent of lilacs. All I could see was blackness. All I could feel was the chill of death. All I could smell was blood.''

Sadness moved over his face. Regret that couldn't be erased by a hand on the arm or by gentle words. Regret that had no cure. ''That's what my life is like, Rees. Taking up a hobby isn't going to solve anything. And dragging you into this hell with me isn't going to solve anything, either.''

She shook her head. Maybe he believed his fate had been sealed, but she didn't. ''When I saw the picture of Dixie in Kane's cell, you told me not to let

Kane win. But *you're* the one letting Kane win, Trent. By pushing everything good out of your life. By letting his darkness overwhelm you, *you* are letting him win."

He turned his head away from her, the muscle working along his jaw.

She gripped his arm as if holding on for dear life. It was *her* turn to explain. *Her* turn to make *him* understand. "It doesn't have to be that way. You don't have to do it all alone. We're strong together. We can get through anything if we're together."

He turned back, his eyes carving into her like hot steel. "You're stronger without me, Rees. You'd be better off never to have known me."

"If you truly believe that, you've already let Kane and all the others like him win."

He leveled a look on her that pierced her heart. "I believe it, Rees," he said, his voice a low rumble. "You should believe it, too."

She closed her eyes. His pain reached deeper inside him than she'd thought. Its roots hooked and tangled with every vital part of him. And nothing she could do could take away that pain. Nothing she could say would make him believe.

Maybe Trent was right. Maybe there were some things you could never fix. Maybe there were some people who never could be saved. God knows her mother had probably been one of those people—drinking herself to death in a final attempt to blot out the disappointments of life. Could Dixie be one of those people, too?

Could Trent?

A chill seeped into Risa and penetrated to the marrow of her bones. Maybe she couldn't save him, nor fix things for him. But she could do something. "I know I can't take away the darkness, Trent. But maybe I can give you a ray of light."

Reaching up, she touched his jaw. His beard stubble rasped rough as sandpaper under her fingertips. Rough and harsh and dark. Everything Trent's life had become. "Let me love you, Trent. Just for tonight. Let me touch you and caress you and love you. You need it. And so do I."

Chapter Twelve

Trent soaked in the tenderness of Rees's fingertips. He'd dreamed of her touch so many times over the past two years. Of her fingers caressing his skin. Of the light shining in her eyes when she looked at him. And now she was here, offering him everything he wanted. Everything he needed. And all he had to do was reach out and take it.

He swallowed into a dry throat. What he wouldn't give to have that light again. To capture it and draw it into his soul. To banish the darkness of his reality for just one night.

A reprieve.

A tremor shook him from the inside out. He ran his hand down her arm, over her shoulder and to her sweet face, trailing his fingertips along her cheek and into the softness of her hair until he cradled the back of her head in his hand.

Her eyes glistened in the darkened room. And when they met his own, the light sparkled in their depths, pure and unshakable.

He couldn't speak, couldn't move. All he could do was look into her eyes. Those strong, brilliant eyes. Eyes that had once fed him, sustained him, kept him going even in the face of darkness.

Eyes that searched his for an answer to her offer.

His heart thumped hard in his chest. His life had become a lonely hell. A study in perseverance. In deprivation. And he couldn't change it. He could never change it.

But he could accept her offer.

He could bask in her wonderful light for one night. He could soak in her energy, store it in his heart and use it to beat back the loneliness. Use it to fortify himself, so he could face the darkness.

She angled her face, lifting her chin. Her lips parted. Inviting. Beseeching. And those eyes. Burning with light, with hope.

Hand still cradling her head, he lowered his face to hers and claimed her lips. Her mouth opened to him, soft and pliant and real. She tasted like sweet honey and felt as soft and comforting as a long, peaceful night. A night with nothing but clear skies and the twinkle of stars overhead. A night uninterrupted by nightmares.

It had been so long since he'd felt this way, since he'd allowed himself to feel anything but anger and regret, the sensation was almost painful in its intensity. Delicious agony.

And he wanted more.

Tearing his lips from hers, he grasped her hand and

led her to the guest room. She followed willingly, eagerly. Her gaze latched on to his as if she too was unable to look away. *Unwilling* to look away.

He led her across the threshold into a room as soft and feminine as Rees herself. Lace dripped from the bed. Candles lined the nightstand. His shoes sank into the thick rug.

The scent of fresh lilacs washed over him in a sweet wave. His stomach constricted. Memories pressed at the back of his eyes, struggling to come to the surface. He pulled her to him. Her softness molded to his body. Her warmth washed over his skin. And instead of memories of blood and obscenity gliding in the lilac scent's wake, its sweetness merely enhanced the fragrance of her hair, her skin. The fragrance of *her*.

And still he wanted more.

Pulling away from her for just a moment, he unhooked his shoulder holster and shrugged out of his shirt.

Rees moved close, her gaze caressing his naked chest. She ran her fingers along his collarbone and over the place where his heart pounded against his ribs.

He grabbed her wrist. He pulled her closer and placed her arm around his neck. Running his hands down her sides and around her back, he encircled her, engulfed her, molded her body to his. Her cotton sweater rubbed his bare chest. Her heat penetrated the fabric and seeped into him like the sun's rays after a long winter chill.

He wanted to touch all of her, feel all of her. He gathered the knitted cotton in his fingers, grasped the ribbing and lifted the sweater over her head.

Moving his fingers along the silk of her skin, he slid the straps of her bra off her shoulders. He released the clasp and pulled the lace and satin free.

Moonlight reached through the lace curtains and accented the perfect roundness of her bare breasts. He covered them with his hands, kneading her softness, teasing her nipples with his fingertips until they tightened into hard nubs.

A moan sounded deep in her chest. A moan of pleasure. A moan of need. Her fingers found the waistband of his slacks. Tentatively she began unbuttoning, as if she expected him to push her away. Again.

She needn't have worried.

Edging her fingers aside, he made short work of stripping off his slacks. His briefs came next. And he stood naked before her.

She ran her hands over his chest, over the plane of his stomach. She closed her fingers around him, her fingers stroking, caressing.

Heat built in his blood. Urgency. He swept his hand over the flat expanse of her belly and pulled at the waistband of her jeans. He wanted to see all of her. Caress all of her. He pushed jeans and panties over her hips and down her legs until they puddled on the floor. Now nothing stood in the way. Nothing separated them. He gathered her body to him and laid her on the bed.

She parted her thighs, nestling him in her softness. Sweet torment pulsed through him. He moved against her wetness, the nub of her desire. Stoking. Building. Igniting. All the time feeding off her lips, breathing in the scent of her hair. Drawing her into his soul.

She gripped his shoulders, her breath caressing his face. Her body tight against him, she tilted her hips. "Please, Trent." Her words were soft, yet full of need.

He buried himself to the hilt in her warmth. She opened to him, moved with him.

He sank into her, then withdrew. Gave himself to her and then pulled away. Each time, she tilted her body against him, beckoning him to join her again. And he complied, surging into her. Stronger with each thrust.

She wrapped her legs around him, pulling him deeper. Deep in the heat. Deep in the flame. Until the blood in his veins was on fire. Until everything was burned away. Everything except her. Except them. And the pure, white light.

BY THE TIME the morning sun reached through the window and awakened Risa from her dreamless sleep, Trent was already gone. She breathed deeply, savoring the scent of his body lingering on the sheets, the memories of his loving lingering in her heart.

He'd needed her last night. Needed her as much as she'd needed him. To soothe his pain. To remind him of what life could be—sweet, loving, gentle. To give him a respite, however short, from the evil and death he lived every day.

The life he would go back to once Kane was captured.

She closed her eyes. Why couldn't Trent see how much better their lives would be if they were together? How much stronger they would both be? If only he had felt the strength surging through them, joining them last night. The strength she had felt.

Maybe he had.

She was almost afraid to hope. Drawing a breath of courage, she opened her eyes, folded back the covers and crawled from the bed. She didn't have time to hole up in bed and wallow in a litany of questions and "if only." Trent had likely been up for hours sorting through FBI files, searching for evidence that could lead to Kane's whereabouts. And she needed to help him. Whether he liked the idea or not.

After grabbing a quick shower, she dried her hair and dressed in a red silk blouse and crisp jeans from her suitcase. Then she headed out to find Trent.

The aroma of coffee drifted to her the moment she opened the guest room door, beckoning her to the kitchen below. She padded down the stairs, the wood steps cool on her bare feet.

She found him in the inn's dining room. A carafe of coffee perched on a mahogany table wide enough to feed a houseful of guests. An empty cup sat on the table as well. Waiting for her. Warmth stirred inside her at his thoughtfulness.

Trent looked up from a file. Cleanly shaved, he wore a starched white dress shirt and pressed tie under his shoulder holster. "Good morning," he said. And though his brow was once again knit with worry and his face tense with concentration, his voice held a note of something she swore hadn't been there yesterday.

"Good morning." She crossed the room and stopped by his side. She wanted to bend down and kiss him like the morning greeting of lovers secure in their love for each other, but she didn't dare. Even if last night had proved to Trent that they were stronger together, that they belonged side by side, what they had shared was too new, too fragile to stand up to the reality of morning.

Contenting herself with laying her hand on his shoulder, she peered at the file spread open on the table in front of him. Police reports stared back at her. Witness interviews.

He closed the flap of the folder, blocking her view.

She bit her bottom lip. She'd wanted to hope something had changed between them last night, something had grown, but maybe she'd hoped too much.

Trent reached down, pulled a fat file from the box at his feet and set it on the table. Swiveling in his chair, he looked up at her. A faint smile crooked his mouth. ''Newspaper clippings to read with your coffee.''

She didn't try to hide the smile that graced her own lips. Something *had* changed last night. However small, however fragile, something was different. ''Thank you.''

He nodded as if he didn't trust his voice. Lifting the carafe, he poured the aromatic liquid into the empty cup, then set the cup on the table next to the file.

She slipped into the chair and took a sip of the coffee. Rich and hot, the brew washed over her taste buds in a welcome wave of flavor. But what she really needed was the dose of caffeine to sharpen her mind. And her eyes. She looked down at the file folder bulging with clippings. Drawing a fortifying breath, she opened the cover and focused on the first article.

The article documented the disappearance of Ashley Dalton, a twenty-year-old biochemistry student who had last been seen by her roommate when she'd left for the bus station. Ashley had been planning to return to the small town she'd grown up in to spend Labor Day weekend with her parents and two younger sisters. When the bus arrived and she wasn't on it, the Daltons had filed a missing person report with the police. The article was very dry and factual, but what hit Risa like a kick to the chest was the photo of the young woman.

Though not exactly beautiful, Ashley Dalton had a

zest for life that came across in the sparkle of her eyes, clearly visible even in the grainy newspaper photo. A zest and sparkle Kane had stolen.

Risa paged through three more entreaties for information on the missing girl before reaching the article proclaiming her body had been found by a deer hunter. Anguish thickened in Risa's throat, but she pushed on. The next article sported several photos covering Ashley's funeral and details of the ongoing investigation. Risa read the article before turning her eyes to the photos.

The first was another photo of Ashley as vibrant as the first. Next to that was a photo of a detective standing in the wooded area where Ashley's body had been found. Risa was about to ask Trent if he recognized the detective when the third photo caught her eye.

It was a shot of the funeral. Ashley's bereaved parents standing at the door of the church, their arms encircling their two younger daughters as if they were afraid the girls would be snatched away from them like their older sister had been.

However, it wasn't the bereaved family that caught Risa's attention, but the sliver of a face hovering in the background. A familiar square-shaped face, his kindly eyes turned down in sorrow.

Duane Levens.

A gasp tore from her lips. Shock stuttered through her mind.

"What? What do you see?" Trent craned his neck to look at the photo.

She angled the clipping toward him and pointed. "It's Duane Levens, the guard at the prison."

Trent stared at the picture. "It sure is."

Questions spun through her mind. What was Duane doing at the funeral of Kane's first victim? Could he have had some sort of tie to Kane? Even back then, two years before the killer was caught?

She squinted to see the grief on Duane's face. Images flooded her mind in a jumble. Duane calling her to the prison to stop her sister from marrying Kane. Duane's eyes hardening in hatred at the sound of Kane's name. Duane's lethal words as he stood with her at the prison entrance. *Scum like that doesn't deserve to live. Not one more day. Not even if it's in a hellhole like this.*

Duane couldn't have helped Kane. He hated Kane. He would never help free a serial killer.

Would he?

I didn't give Kane anything. The only thing I wanted to give him was a bullet in the head.

A cold finger traveled up Risa's spine.

Trent raised his gaze to hers, the look in his eyes telling her his mind was traveling a similar path. Without saying a word, he bent and shuffled through the files in the box at his feet. He withdrew a file and spread it open on the table.

He scanned through the pages with narrowed eyes. Finally he plucked a report from the stack and placed it in front of Risa. "Ashley Dalton had a boyfriend.

The police thought he might be a suspect for a while. But they cleared him.''

She looked down at the paper. The name of the subject interviewed stared back at her in black and white.

Duane Levens.

She raised her eyes to Trent's. It was clear to her now. Duane's attempt to keep Dixie from marrying Kane. His hatred for the killer. His comments about Kane deserving to die. It all made sense. ''Kane killed Duane's girlfriend. And Duane wants revenge.''

TRENT GRIPPED the steering wheel hard and swung the car through the twists and curves in the road. With each foot of road whirring under the tires, the bed-and-breakfast faded farther and farther into the past, only the tangle of forest visible now in the rearview mirror.

In the passenger seat next to him, Rees held on, one hand on the door handle, one hand on the dash, the seat belt holding her securely in her seat. She hadn't said two words since she'd discovered the newspaper clipping of Levens at Ashley Dalton's funeral. She'd simply gotten ready to leave while he'd made arrangements to suspend the trap until they had time to check out Levens.

Damn Duane Levens.

It was bad enough he'd helped a serial killer escape in some misguided and botched attempt at vigilante justice. But that wasn't all he'd done. His actions had caused two deaths and still threatened Dixie's life.

And he'd put Rees's life in jeopardy. For that alone, Trent wanted to close his fingers around the guard's neck and squeeze.

He raked a hand through his hair and drew a breath of sanity. He couldn't let emotion cloud his thinking. He had to focus on how to use Levens to find Kane, not on choking the life out of him. He had to do whatever he could to save Dixie. He had to do whatever he could to keep Rees out of Kane's clutches.

He glanced at her again. Even with the discovery of Levens's involvement in Kane's escape, the urgency to question him and the details of this case swamping his mind, he couldn't keep his thoughts from straying to what had happened between them last night. He could still smell the sweet fragrance of her hair, still taste the ripeness of her breasts, still feel the brilliance of her light enveloping him, infusing him. He'd been like a starving man at a banquet table, filling himself with her essence, her energy.

He couldn't get enough last night. Hell, who was he fooling? He couldn't get enough *now*. Even having her in the seat beside him filled him with incredible warmth, incredible light.

And that was what worried him. Because now that he'd basked in her light again, how would he go back to living without it?

He forced his eyes to the road in front of him, his mind to the matter at hand. He couldn't answer that question. Not now. Now he could only find Kane. Find Dixie.

And hope to hell Levens could give them some answers.

Drops of rain spattered the windshield, turning the winding road ahead into a glistening black snake, the trees whizzing past into a blurred mosaic of green and brown. Trent switched on the windshield wipers. The rhythmic swish over glass marked each minute and each mile ticking by. Reaching the end of the road, he performed a rolling stop and checked traffic before gunning the car out onto the highway.

Once on the straighter road, Rees loosened her grip and turned to him. "Will the FBI beat us to Duane's house?"

"Probably." He'd prefer confronting Levens at the prison, a much more controlled and predictable environment. But the guard had the day off, so Trent didn't have a choice. "The local sheriff's department will also be there. Levens should be safely detained by the time we arrive."

Her lips straightened in a determined line. A little crease furrowed her forehead between arched brows. "Let me talk to him, Trent. He'll talk to me. I know he will. He'll help me save Dixie."

He gritted his teeth. He didn't like the idea of dragging Rees into this mess, but she was right. Levens liked her. He'd made that clear when he'd opened up to her the last time they'd questioned him. Besides, if Levens was any kind of a man, he would feel guilty for the grief his actions had caused Rees. And the danger he'd caused her sister. If anyone could get him to confess what he'd done and what he knew about Kane, Rees could. "All right. You question Levens."

She nodded resolutely, and he couldn't miss the small smile that curled the corners of her lips. "We'll work together, Trent."

Together. Better. Stronger.

He raked a hand through his hair. He couldn't think that way. He could think only of doing his job. Finding Kane. Saving lives. He could focus only on what was real.

He concentrated on making a sharp turn off the highway and onto another winding country road. "Damn. Didn't they build any straight roads in this part of the state?"

The dark green sedan blocking the next intersection marked Levens's driveway as clearly as a neon sign. Trent pulled into the driveway and hit the brakes. Plucking his ID and badge from his suit jacket, he opened his window and flashed them at the deputy.

The deputy nodded in greeting. "Special Agent Donatelli told me to expect you."

"Is the suspect in custody?"

"Yes. He's in the house. Go ahead." The deputy moved to the side and waved Trent around the parked car.

Fastening his ID to the outside of his suit jacket, Trent shifted into gear and followed the deputy's direction. The car bumped and dipped through the shallow ditch flanking the drive. Once the tires hit gravel, he accelerated toward the small house.

A bevy of cars lined the driveway, their roofs and hoods glistening in the now-steady rain. Sheriff's deputies and FBI agents swarmed house and grounds.

Trent pulled the car up to the garage and stopped. He gave Rees a nod. "Let's go."

She pursed her lips and opened the car door. Once out of the car, she fell into step behind him.

They climbed the steps to the front door of the raised ranch, cold rain falling steadily on their heads and shoulders. Two agents flanked the door. "They're waiting for you in the living room," one of the agents said.

Trent nodded, and he and Rees ducked inside.

The overcast sky was bright compared to the gloom inside the house. Trent paused for a moment to let his eyes adjust. Dark paneling covered the walls of the entry and stretched up the half-staircase to the living room. Fishing rods and tackle gathered in a pile just inside the door.

He guided Rees around the fishing gear, and they climbed the stairs to a room decorated with photos of men proudly showing off their catches.

Levens stood in a dim corner of the room. He shook his head slowly, his brow furrowed as if he didn't understand why anyone would want to do this to him. Hands secured behind his back in cuffs, he towered over the agents around him. Only Donatelli came close to matching the hulking guard in height.

Levens stared past Trent, his eyes on Rees. A look of shame so deep it was painful passed over his coarse features. He quickly looked away and focused on his feet. "I'm sorry, Professor."

Rees stepped in front of Levens. The guard was at least a foot taller than she, but he didn't seem half as tall in stature. Her back straight and strong, she peered up into the guard's eyes. "What happened, Duane?"

The guard shook his big head. "I didn't mean for him to take your sister. You got to believe I never meant for that to happen."

"I know," Risa said, her voice tight. "What I don't know is why you helped him."

Levens gnashed his teeth so hard Trent could swear he heard the enamel creak with the pressure. "I didn't help him. I would *never* help him."

"You helped him escape, Duane."

Color bloomed on the guard's cheeks, but he kept his mouth shut tight.

"Why did you do it?" Rees prodded. "So you wouldn't go to prison yourself when you killed him?"

Levens raised his eyes to hers. Tears glimmered on his lower lashes. His chin trembled as he fought for control. "Ashley didn't deserve what he did to her. I wanted to make him pay. He should pay."

"He was in prison, Duane. He *was* paying."

"You call that paying? Three squares a day, television, exercise equipment, books? Special favors from the guards? A beautiful girl to marry him?" Breath chugged in and out of his flared nostrils. Passion stained his cheeks. "He deserves a little of the hell he put Ashley and those other girls through. He deserves to die."

"Maybe so." Rees shook her head, her eyes sad, dark as bruises. "All I know is that while he was in prison, Dixie was safe."

Levens flinched. "I didn't mean for him to get loose. I didn't mean for him to kidnap your sister. I wanted him in pain. I wanted him dead."

"So what went wrong?"

"I let him into the garbage area, and then I waited for him at the garbage truck's first stop after the prison. But when the truck arrived, he wasn't in it anymore. He got out somehow. He had to have gotten out while the truck was still moving."

"It didn't occur to you that he'd bail out early?" Trent didn't even try to keep the disbelief from his voice.

"He shouldn't have been able to. It's straight highway from the prison to the next stop. Fifty-five miles an hour. He shouldn't have been able to jump out at that speed. He sure as hell shouldn't have been able to walk away from a jump like that." The guard brought his gaze back to Rees. He stared at her with sunken eyes. Vacant eyes. As if his soul had been burned away by hatred, and nothing was left but an empty shell. "I'm sorry."

A bitter taste tinged Trent's mouth. He understood what Levens had done. Understood the reasons behind it. The hatred, the regret, the failure. He understood all of it. Far too well. "Do you have any idea where Kane might be now?"

"No." The guard closed his eyes in defeat. "If I did, I would have killed him already."

The chirp of a cell phone cut through the heavy thud of disappointment in Trent's stomach. He reached for the phone clipped to his belt, but the light indicating an incoming call wasn't flashing. "It's not mine."

Donatelli looked up from his own phone and shook his head.

The phone chirped again. This time the sound seemed clearly to be coming from Rees's direction.

"I forgot I had it with me." She dipped her hand into her jacket pocket and retrieved her phone. Turning it on, she held it to her ear. "Hello?"

Unease pricked Trent's skin like a thousand tiny needles.

Rees swallowed hard. Color drained from her face. "Dixie, is that you?"

Chapter Thirteen

Risa's pulse thundered in her ears. She clutched the phone tighter, as if it were Dixie herself and if Risa were to let go, she'd lose her sister forever. She lifted her eyes to Trent's.

He moved to her side in one quick step. Putting an arm around her shoulder, he pulled her close and pressed his head next to the phone.

She angled it away from her ear so he could hear. "Where are you, Dix? Tell me where you are and I'll come and get you."

"No." Though she whispered, fear pulsed from her voice as clearly as if she'd screamed. "You can't come and get me. He wants you, Risa. He's after you."

He *was* after her, but he would kill Dixie first. Fear pulsed in Risa's ears like the steady beat of a drum. Fear for her sister. "Where are you calling from? Where is he now?"

"He's outside. He doesn't know I'm calling."

Horrible images of what Kane would do if he found

Dixie on the phone crashed through her. "Are you sure he won't walk in on you?"

"I'm sure."

"Can you get out of there, Dixie? Can you run?"

"He's out in the yard. He'll see me and hunt me down. That's what he likes to do. That's what he— Oh, Risa." Her voice erupted in anguish. Sobs broke through the static. "I really screwed up this time."

"It's okay, Dix."

"No, it's not okay. I thought he loved me. I really did."

The agony in her sister's voice ripped her heart. Guilt throbbed in her chest. "I know, Dix. I'm so sorry. If I hadn't—"

"It wasn't your fault, Rees."

"I abandoned you."

"And I blamed you for that for a long time. But I was wrong." Dixie's sobs quieted to sniffled tears, and her voice grew clearer, more determined. "If anything happens to me, I don't want you blaming yourself."

"Nothing's going to happen, Dix. I won't let it."

"You have no control over what happens now, Risa, so just hear me out." Dixie's voice took on a note of command despite her tears, a note of strength Risa had never heard from her before. "It wasn't your fault our mother drank. It wasn't your fault my father didn't love me. And it wasn't your fault I wanted Dryden to love me so badly I didn't see him for what he really is. So no blaming yourself anymore, you hear?''

She couldn't stop a little smile of pride from creeping over her lips. Dixie had been through a hell no one should ever have to experience. But instead of letting it beat her, she'd grown stronger. And she would come out of it. Risa would see to it. "Tell me where you are, Dix."

"Promise me you won't blame yourself. No matter what happens."

No matter what happens. Risa closed her eyes, trying to beat down the images that phrase evoked. "I promise. Now where are you?"

"I can't tell you. You'll come after me. That's just what Dryden wants." Her voice rang with determination. "Is Trent with you?"

"Yes." Risa opened her eyes and looked at Trent. He returned her pointed gaze. "Will you tell Trent where you are?"

"Put him on the phone. And Risa?"

"What, Dix?"

"I love you."

Risa's throat tightened, and tears stung her eyes. "I love you, too, Dix." Swallowing hard, she handed the phone to Trent.

His steel-gray eyes drilled into her, penetrating, assessing, as if he knew how much turning Dixie over to him cost her. He held the phone to his ear. "This is Trent, Dixie. I'll take Rees to the Grantsville police station where she'll be safe. She won't come after you. I guarantee it. It will just be me, the FBI and the sheriff's department. Now where are you?"

TRENT PULLED THE CAR in front of the police station's front door and stopped. He stared straight out the windshield, careful not to let his eyes stray to Rees sitting beside him in the passenger seat.

Teeth gritted and arms folded across her chest, she sat stone still beside him. Anger and desperation pulsed in her every movement, her every breath. "I need to be there, Trent. For Dixie." She spat the words at him for the tenth time on the drive to the station.

"I keep telling you, Rees. I'm going to take care of Dixie. And I'm going to take care of you, too."

"By shutting me away?"

"Yes."

"But you said yourself the whole FBI and sheriff's department are going to be at the house where Dixie is. I'd be plenty safe there."

"Amid the gunfire? No, I don't think so." Just the thought of her around the kind of operation the FBI and sheriff's department would set up to rescue Dixie and catch Kane made Trent's shoulders clench with anxiety. And that was if everything went according to plan and they were able to subdue the serial killer and get Dixie out of the house alive. If they weren't— He shook the thought from his mind. He couldn't even consider the ramifications if something went wrong. "I don't want you there."

"And that's the crux of the matter, isn't it? You don't want me with you. Even after all that's happened."

How wrong she was. He wanted her there. He wanted her with him always. But that was impossible. "I want you where I know you'll be safe. And that place is here with the Grantsville police surrounding you."

"Away from you."

"Yes."

"Didn't you learn anything last night?"

"Last night?" Surprise jolted him and echoed in his voice. "What has last night got to do with any of this?"

"We are stronger together, Trent. I'd hoped you'd felt that last night."

He had felt a lot of things last night. Amazing things. Last night was a fantasy. A dream. And if there was anything he had learned—if there was anything that had been drilled into his soul in the past years—it was that fantasies and dreams couldn't last. He had to deal with reality. "Last night was wonderful. But it doesn't change anything."

"So you didn't feel stronger when we were together? Is that what you're saying?"

He ground his teeth. "*You* believe we are stronger together, Rees. Not me. I've never believed that."

"And you never will."

A cold chill spread over his skin. "I guess not."

She nodded slowly, staring into his eyes as if

searching for a sliver of hesitation, a shred of a chance that she could change his mind.

He met her probing gaze. She wouldn't find what she was looking for. He had nothing to offer her. And no matter how much she wanted things to be different—no matter how much *he* wanted it—he couldn't change the way things were.

Finally, she looked away. She opened the car door, climbed out into the steady rain and closed the door behind her. Turning back for a moment, she peered at him through the rivulets of rain running down the window like tears. The light still burned in her eyes, as strong and pure as ever before. But he could no longer feel its warmth, no longer touch the rays of hope, no longer bask in its brilliance.

He swallowed into an aching throat and watched her walk into the police station.

RAIN DRIPPED off Trent's hair and trickled down the back of his neck. He stifled a shiver, training his eyes on the Tudor-style house barely visible through the new sprouts of leaves on the bushes he crouched behind. No sound came from the house or surrounding neighborhood. Nothing but the patter of cold rain on leaves.

Damn fine day for a hostage situation.

Provided Kane still had a hostage inside. Provided he hadn't already killed Dixie.

Trent raked his fingers through his rain-soaked hair. He *had* to bring Dixie out alive. He *had* to deliver her safely to Rees. He couldn't give Rees the life, the happiness she deserved, but he could deliver her sister from Kane's clutches. And he could keep Rees safe.

Sheriff's deputies and FBI silently moved into place around the house. Trent moved into position near the front door. Drawing his Glock from his shoulder holster, he fitted it into his hand. The grip felt comfortable, secure. Normally, he wouldn't be among the first to go in, but this case was different. He wasn't about to sit on the sidelines and watch.

Donatelli and other agents fell in beside him.

Two agents at the front door positioned the battering ram. At Donatelli's signal, the crash of breaking glass shattered the air from the rear of the house, followed by a small explosion.

Trent tensed at the sound of the incendiary device used to divert Kane's attention from the front door. The agents near him drew back the battering ram. With a single heave, they drove it home. Wood cracked. The door flew open. Trent sprang to his feet and burst through the opening. He flattened against the inside wall. Armed men flowed in behind him.

Trent's heart thundered in his ears, pumping adrenaline through his veins. He squinted, willing his eyes to adjust to the darkness in the house. Taking turns advancing while the others provided cover, he and the other agents moved down the hall and fanned out into the rooms.

He was the first to round the corner into what appeared to be the master bedroom. A prone form lay spread-eagle on the wide bed, wrists and ankles secured to the headboard and footboard by speaker wire. Trent's heart jolted.

Dixie.

She lay unmoving, her skin deathly pale against the dark cloud of her hair and the dirty blue blouse and tattered jeans she wore. Fear jolted through him. He couldn't be too late. He couldn't be. He raced to the side of the bed.

She turned her face and stared up at him with glassy eyes. "Trent?"

Relief pounded through him. Thank God, she was alive. "You're going to be okay, Dixie. You're going home." He quickly untied her wrists and helped her into a sitting position.

She was thinner than he remembered. Frail. And she clung to him like a frightened kitten. "Oh, Trent. I'm so sorry. I'm so sorry." A fresh torrent streamed from her eyes and dampened the shoulder of his bullet-proof vest.

He smoothed his hand over her tangled hair. She looked so much like Rees now that her hair was dark again. He'd never realized how much the sisters looked like each other. "You're safe. I have you. Now where's Kane?"

"I don't know. I think he left. He always ties me up when he leaves. Where's Risa?"

"I took her to the police station like I told you on the phone. She's safe."

Dixie nodded, gasping for breath between sobs.

Donatelli strode into the room, his gaze zeroing in on Trent. "She's right. Kane's gone. And there are no cars in the garage."

"Damn." Unease clamped the back of Trent's neck. Kane's disappearance just before they arrived was too neat, too convenient. He turned back to Dixie. Grasping her shoulders, he held her far enough away to see into her eyes. "Did Kane say anything about where he was going?"

She clung to his gaze. "No. He didn't tell me anything. He just kept saying what he was going to do to me. What he was going to do to Risa." She closed her eyes, fighting back another wave of sobs. "He killed a woman, Trent. He hunted her down and killed her."

Trent glanced to the woods surrounding the house. Even with the leaves sprouting on the trees, he could see the outline of the two-story house looming next door. Kane couldn't have staged his hunt of Farrentina Hamilton here. Not with the neighbors so close. Not without them hearing Farrentina's screams. And Kane wouldn't have gagged her. Not Kane. He would want to hear her screams, her fear. Gagging her would have stolen his whole purpose behind the hunt.

No. He had staged his hunt someplace else. And if Trent found Kane's hunting grounds, he might find Kane. "Where did this hunt take place, Dixie? Where did he take the woman?"

"I'm not sure. It was a cabin. He tied me inside

while he killed her.'' She squeezed her eyes shut and shook her head, as if trying to dislodge the memory.

A cabin. In a sparsely populated area. ''Were there photos in the cabin or anything that might have had the owner's name on it?''

''No. But Dryden talked about the owner.''

A fresh shot of adrenaline pumped into Trent's bloodstream. ''By name?''

''No. He just said the owner would bust a gut if he knew we were there.''

''Bust a gut? Why?''

''Because he hated Dryden. And Dryden had used him. To get out of prison, I think.''

Levens.

The fishing equipment and photographs he'd seen at the guard's house flashed into Trent's mind. Levens must have a fishing cabin. A cabin Kane had found out about somehow. And after Kane had foiled the guard's vigilante plan, he couldn't resist rubbing Levens's nose in the victory by using the guard's secluded retreat as his private hunting grounds.

Trent turned to Donatelli. ''Levens must have a fishing cabin in the area.''

Donatelli nodded. ''We're on it.''

Trent turned back to Dixie. ''When did Kane leave?''

She had only to consider the question for a split second. ''Right after I talked to you on the phone.''

''*After* you talked to me?'' A cold hand of fear

gripped his gut. "Could he have heard what we said?"

She shook her head. "He was outside. I snuck into the bedroom to use the phone. He didn't know I called." Her eyes moved back and forth, scanning Trent's face. "He couldn't have known. He would have been very angry if he'd known. He would have stopped me."

Trent wasn't so sure. The ache assaulting his neck spread into his shoulders and radiated down his back. Kane didn't make mistakes. He was far too clever to leave Dixie with access to a phone unless he intended for her to call for help. And Kane would know exactly who Dixie would call if she got the chance. "Is there another extension in the house?"

"In the kitchen." Dixie's eyes grew wide. "You don't think—" She held her hand to her mouth.

"That he was listening?" He forced the words through a throat already closing with panic. "Yes, I do. And he knows exactly where Rees is."

Exactly where Trent had left her.

For her own safety.

RISA SLUMPED in her now-familiar chair in the hallway of the Grantsville police station. Silence echoed through the tiny building, broken by nothing but the tap of an ancient typewriter in the office down the hall. She balled her hands into fists and struggled to control the tension coiling in her muscles like a spring ready to snap. She hated not knowing what was going on. Hated the endless questions spiraling through her mind with no answers in sight. Had they reached Dixie in time? Was she safe? Had they captured Kane?

She dug her cell phone out of her jacket pocket and checked to make sure it was turned on for the hundredth time in the past hour. Surely Trent would call her soon and let her know what was going on. Surely his need to exclude her from his life didn't extend to not keeping her informed.

Trent.

She caught her bottom lip between her teeth. The emptiness throbbing in her chest intensified with each beat of her heart. When he had insisted on leaving her at the police station, she'd had to face what she'd feared all along. He would never see that he could have a better life. He would never give them a chance. He would never believe they were stronger together.

She probably should have seen it all along. She *had* seen it, but she hadn't wanted to give up. She hadn't wanted to accept that she and Trent would never be together—could never be together.

Now she had no choice. He had made the choice for her. And there was nothing she could do to change it.

Trent would go back to his lonely life. And she would struggle on rebuilding hers. Alone. There would be no happy ending. Not for them.

But there might be a happy ending for Dixie.

She tangled her fingers together in her lap and mouthed a silent prayer.

A door swung open into the hall and the fresh face of Grantsville's police chief peered out. "How are you holding up, Professor?"

She shot to her feet, barely preventing herself from lunging at him and demanding answers. "Have you heard anything?"

"Not a word." Chief John Rook offered an apologetic smile.

She nodded and lowered herself back into her chair.

"Sorry."

"It's not your fault. I'm just a little jumpy." With great effort, she managed to bring an answering smile to her lips. The police chief had been kind enough to house her in his station and provide her with protection. The last thing she needed to do to repay his dedication was jump all over him.

"I'll let you know the moment I hear anything new. Don't worry."

"Thanks, John."

"No problem." His grin widened, and he nodded in an awkward attempt to be reassuring. "Listen, I'm going to step out to Lionel's Grill for a couple of their special Black Forest sandwiches. Can I get you one?"

Sandwiches. Lunch. She glanced at the clock. It was past one o'clock. She had totally lost track of time. "No thanks. I'm not hungry."

"You sure? You gotta eat."

She shook her head. "I'm sure. Thanks anyway."

"I'll get you one just in case you change your mind." He gestured to the front door of the station. "It's only two doors down. I'll be back before you know I'm gone. Don is in the back office. He'll let you know if any news comes in."

"Thanks."

He gave her a gentle smile and strode out the front door.

She slumped in her chair. She hated being so powerless. So utterly helpless. She hated not knowing. She hated having to sit and wait.

And it was so quiet. Even the plunk of Don's search-and-peck typing had stopped in the office. Nothing to distract her. Nothing to still her wild tumble of thoughts. Thoughts of what was happening this minute while she sat in this hallway alone. Thoughts of what would happen in the future, after Kane was caught, after Trent's role was over, after he left her alone, struggling to patch her shattered life back together.

Struggling to heal her broken heart.

A thump sounded from outside the door to the station. The door that Rook had just walked through.

She straightened in her chair, trying to identify the sound. Something hitting the wall of the station? Or, more likely, the distant slam of a car door?

Could it be Trent? Was he back? Did he have Dixie?

Her heartbeat picked up its pace. She rose from her chair just as the front door swung open.

Blue eyes glittered like shards of ice. A smile slithered over thin lips. And one fist balled around the handle of a knife, the gleam of its blade muted by smears of fresh blood.

Somewhere in the back of her mind, she heard the radio squawk from the back office. Trent's voice shouted over the airwaves. A warning that Kane was on his way.

Chapter Fourteen

Fear screamed in Risa's ears.

"Hello, Risa. Miss me?" Kane's silky voice rang with a note of sadistic glee. He stepped toward her. His athletic shoes, wet from the outdoors, squeaked on the tile floor.

She stood riveted to the spot, her legs frozen, her mind paralyzed. Kane. Here. Coming for her.

"I sure missed you." His grin widened. He took another step forward. "Dixie is a nice girl, but she's lacking in conversational skills."

Terror clogged her throat, bitter as bile. Finally getting her feet to move, she lurched backward, running into the legs of her chair and almost going down in a heap.

"Of course, maybe my memory of you is a little enhanced. You don't seem to be very talkative today. What's the matter? Cat got your tongue?"

Regaining her balance, she backed away from him, step after step, groping for the wall behind her. She had to find help.

"I sure hope your loss of speech isn't permanent. I was looking forward to hearing you beg for mercy. I can't wait to see how good you are at begging."

Scream. She had to scream. She forced a sound past her lips. A gurgle echoed through the tiny station, then a piercing shriek.

"Music to my ears." He threw his head back as if exulting in the sound. "No one can hear you. Just me. But I appreciate the private concert."

No one— Police Chief Rook? Don, the cop typing in the back office? Had Kane killed them both? Slit their throats like he had Deputy Perry's? She looked to the front door, desperately willing Rook to walk in, gun in hand.

The door remained closed—the entire station silent except for the relentless pounding of her heart.

"Don't you think I would take care of the loose ends before I set foot inside that door? I've planned for this meeting, Risa darling. I've planned every detail."

Alarm spun through her mind in a dizzying whirl. She grasped the wall behind her and willed her mind to clear. She had to stay levelheaded. She had to focus.

"I don't want any interruptions." He lowered one eyelid in a wink. "We have too much catching up to do."

Her mind groped for a sliver of hope. She'd heard Trent's voice on the radio in the office. She'd heard him say the police were on the way. Trent was on the way.

But would he make it in time?

She eyed the blade in Kane's hand. No. He'd never reach her. Not before Kane did. She was alone. She had to get away from Kane herself. She had to run for it.

She tensed the muscles in her legs, ready to spring. There had to be a back door to the station. A door she could escape through. It was her only chance. Whirling, she dashed down the hall.

Kane's shoes squeaked into motion behind her. Faster. Closer.

Grabbing the door frame, she whipped into the office. A body slumped over a typewriter. Blood oozed red and wet down the desk.

Risa's stomach retched.

Beyond the body, a neon Exit sign gleamed. Her escape. Her only chance. She forced her feet to keep moving.

Kane turned into the office. Two steps behind her. One step.

She reached for the doorknob. Her fingers brushed cold metal.

His hand grabbed her hair. Her head snapped back. Momentum slammed her into the door. She fell, her knees hitting the hard tile.

Pulling her to her feet by her hair, he yanked her back against his body. A cold edge of steel pressed against her neck. "Where were you going? We have so much to talk about.'' His breath fanned the side of her cheek. Mint. As if he'd freshened it just for her.

A shudder racked her body, a convulsion she couldn't control.

He had her. Oh God, Kane had her.

''You don't seem happy to see me, Risa. You don't seem happy at all. Why is that?''

Pain wrenched her neck and throbbed in her knees and scalp.

''Is it because you like to be in control? Is it because you like to set a guy up and then humiliate him? Do you like to play those games?'' Fingers still entwined in her hair and blade pressed to her throat, he pulled her back past the body slumped over the desk and toward the door. ''Well, I have a game for you, sweet cheeks. And you're going to love it.''

TRENT REACHED under John Rook's bloody body. Finding the column of his neck, he felt for a pulse. A soft, irregular rhythm beat under his fingertips. ''He's still alive. Barely. Call for an ambulance. Now.''

''On their way,'' someone shouted.

Wiley raced up beside him and fell to his knees. ''I've got him.''

Trent didn't argue. Leaving Rook in the sergeant's hands, he scrambled to his feet and rushed into the police station.

The station swarmed with FBI and deputies. Donatelli stood in the center of the entry hall. He spun to face Trent. His eyes were dark. His face heavily lined. "The cop in the office is dead. Throat cut. Name's Don Largent."

Fear consolidated in Trent's gut, hardening into a leaden mass. "Rees?"

Donatelli shook his head. "She's not here. There's no sign of her."

Kane had Rees.

Dizziness twisted through him. He shook his head, willing it away. He had to focus. He had to concentrate.

"We put an APB out for the black-and-white he stole." Donatelli's face sharpened with concern. "There's no sign that he killed her, Burnell. She's probably still alive."

Of course she was still alive. Killing her was only part of Kane's fantasy. And acting out the fantasy was paramount to Kane. Especially acting out the fantasy with Rees. "He's going to hunt her."

"The Levens cabin?"

"Maybe." He hoped Kane had taken her to Levens's fishing cabin. He hoped it was that easy. "Have the men you sent reached the cabin yet?"

Donatelli shook his silver head. "Not yet."

Trent spun on his heel and headed for the door. "Call me when they do. I'm on my way."

He burst out the door. Negotiating around the ambulance and emergency medical team attending to Rook, he ran to his car, gravel crunching under his boots. Levens's cabin was miles away. In another county. He had no time to lose.

Once inside his car, he pulled onto the highway, pressing the accelerator to the floor. His mind raced, fast as spinning wheels on pavement.

When Kane left the ranch house, he'd known the FBI was on its way. He'd known they would find Dixie. He'd counted on it. He'd planned they would waste their time staking out the house, evacuating the surrounding neighbors, setting up their assault. He'd counted on the operation draining all the deputies and agents from the police station, leaving only the normal skeleton crew of Grantsville officers. And he knew that once they found Dixie, she would tell them about the cabin. She would tell them he'd left right after her phone call. And they'd rush back to the police station to find Rook's and the other officer's bodies.

And they'd find Rees gone.

He'd been ahead of them every step of the way. So why would he take her back to the cabin? Why would he take her to the place they would look first?

He wouldn't.

He wouldn't take her to the cabin. Trent was sure of it. But if not the cabin, where?

Trent didn't have a clue. And unless he came up with something, and fast, Rees was dead.

His head pounded. His heart ached so hard it took his breath away. If ever there was a time for him to feel what Kane felt, to know what Kane would do, to be part of Kane, that time was now. He had to think. He had to feel. He had to see.

He swung the car to the highway's shoulder and shifted into Park. Covering his burning face with cold fingers, he closed his eyes.

He knew Kane. He could think like the killer thought. He could feel what the killer felt. Surely he could come up with the place Kane would take Rees—the object of his obsession—to play out the fantasy he'd been creating in his mind since he'd read her humiliating words in the psychiatric journal.

When Kane had killed his wife, he'd taken her to his hunting cabin in the north woods. A place where he had escaped the humiliation of his life. A place where he hunted prey weaker than himself. A place where he was king and master.

He no longer had any such place.

Trent opened his eyes and raked a hand through his hair. The answer had to be there. Buried somewhere in Kane's mind. Somewhere in his past behavior. Born from his insecurities, his desires, his twisted black heart.

He'd taken Farrentina to Levens's cabin to stage his hunt. He'd stayed in the cabin because he knew the guard would "bust a gut," as Dixie had said. After the hunt, he'd displayed Farrentina's body on Rees's front porch. He'd wanted to scare her. To drive home his mastery over women that looked like her. And then the locket they'd found, the photo of Rees inside. His way of announcing to law enforcement that Rees was already his. That he was going to steal her out from under their noses. And with his bold entrance into the hotel, his slashing of Deputy Perry's throat—he'd almost succeeded.

This time he had.

Trent gripped the steering wheel until his knuckles ached. Kane had Rees. But Trent couldn't let the killer succeed.

He wouldn't.

He forced himself to concentrate. The answer was there, he could feel it. He just had to dig deep enough to find it. Before Kane had gone to prison, his choice for a hunting site had been deeply personal. A place he felt strong. A place he was the master. And he'd dumped the bodies in secret locations. Locations they weren't likely to be casually stumbled upon. Ones that would afford him the privacy to return and relive his fantasies even weeks after the kill without danger of being caught.

All that had changed after he'd broken from prison. Now it seemed his choices were all designed to exact revenge. He'd killed Farrentina at the fishing cabin to pay Duane back for his hatred and the power he held behind the prison walls. He'd dropped her body on Rees's front step to hurt Rees. And he'd taken her from the police station to thumb his nose at law enforcement. And following that path of behavior, Kane would choose the place he would take Rees in the same way.

Who would Kane revenge himself against this time? Who would Rees's death hurt the most?

Trent's heart stilled in his chest. A pain erupted behind his eyes, so sharp he lowered his forehead against the steering wheel. He knew just who Rees's death would hurt the most. And so did Kane.

Him.

He slammed the butt of his hands on the steering wheel. Pain thundered up his arm. Righteous pain. He knew where Kane had taken Rees. He knew right where the killer planned to let her loose, hunt her, kill her and display her body.

But Trent would be damned if he would let the killer do any of those things.

He may have lost a part of himself to Kane two years ago, but he wasn't going to lose Rees. He'd die first.

And he'd take that murdering son of a bitch with him.

FEAR CONSTRICTED Risa's chest, making it hard to breathe, hard to think. Hands bound in front of her by handcuffs Kane had stolen from Police Chief Rook, she stared out the rain-spotted windshield at the canopy of trees stretching over the road and struggled to force the images of Farrentina Hamilton's body from her mind. She couldn't think of what Kane would do to her if she didn't get away from him. She had to focus. She had to play this right.

If she didn't, she was dead.

Next to her, Kane draped a hand over the wheel of the stolen police car and wove around the curves as if he were on a Sunday drive without a care in the world.

But she knew differently.

She could feel the violence coiled under his skin. She could see the contempt burning in his eyes every time he looked at her.

She could taste the fear, like rusted tin creeping up her throat, gagging her, choking her.

The leafy canopy opened before them, revealing the Victorian bed and breakfast she'd left just this morning. But unlike the warm glow that filled the house this morning, now it was dark, the windows staring like empty, soulless eyes. Rain glistened off the steep roof.

"Nice place. The FBI has a more generous expense account than I ever imagined." Kane's thin lips twisted into a smile. He turned to stare at her, his eyes as cold and deadly as the blade sheathed by his side. "Kind of them to clear out and leave the place to us now, isn't it?"

She jutted her chin forward and glared at him. "The FBI is going to figure out where we are, Kane."

"You think Burnell is going to figure it out, huh?" A bitter laugh sounded deep in his throat. "I hope he does. And I hope he likes the display I have planned for him."

The image of Farrentina displayed on her front steps once again flashed through Risa's mind. Kane

would display *her* body, too. Display her so Trent
would find her. So the image of her mutilated corpse
would haunt him the rest of his days. Anger and fear
throbbed in her stomach. Nausea lapped at her self-
control.

"Would you like me to tell you about it?" Violence reached from his gaze and traveled over her skin
like an uncontrolled shudder.

She bit the inside of her bottom lip until the coppery tang of blood flooded her mouth, drowning out
the taste of fear. She knew Kane's game. He wanted
to see terror in her eyes. Hear it in her screams. Revel
in it. Feed on it.

She'd be damned if she'd give him the satisfaction.

Taking a firm grip on the trembling in her stomach,
she pursed her lips together and stared straight ahead
through the windshield. The hard metal edges of the
handcuffs securing her wrists bit into her skin. Her
scalp and knees throbbed with each rapid pulse of her
heart. But none of it mattered. She wouldn't let it. He
could say whatever the hell he pleased. She wouldn't
play her role in his fantasy.

He stopped the police car at the foot of the path
leading to the bed-and-breakfast's front door and
turned toward her. "Don't want to hear about my
exhibit, eh?" Reaching a hand to her face, he ran a
cold finger along one cheekbone.

She tensed to keep the tremor of revulsion from
claiming her.

"Oh, Risa. So brave. So in control. You always

have to control everything, don't you? That's your problem, you know. You're a controlling bitch. Even your dim-witted sister picked up on that.''

She continued to stare straight ahead, letting his words hit her and bounce off. She couldn't let him under her skin. She couldn't let him drill into her insecurities. She couldn't let him hit the well of fear surging inside her.

He moved his hand into her hair, tangling the strands around his fingers. ''Well, you might as well give it up. You might as well let go. Because I'm in control now.'' His fingers tightened, pulling her hair.

Pain seared her scalp. Her eyes watered.

Opening the door, he forced her across the seat and out the door after him.

Her bruised knees hit pavement with stinging force. A cry of pain tore from her lips.

He peered down at her, eyes gleaming. ''Get up.'' Still gripping her by a fistful of hair, he yanked her to her feet and pulled her behind him, across the wet lawn.

Limping, she struggled to keep up. Blood oozed from her knees and stuck to the torn denim of her jeans. Her scalp burned as if it were on fire. Cold rain drenched her hair and trickled into her eyes.

He stopped at the edge of the woods and pulled her against him, his face just inches from hers, his eyes narrowing with cold fury. His breath fanned her, sharp and fresh with mint. ''I'm not as inadequate as you thought, am I? Not as inadequate as you described in your article."

She drew in a shaky gasp. "It was a psychological profile, Kane. It wasn't personal." Even as the words left her lips, she knew she had made a mistake.

He answered her with a slow, carnivorous smile. "Of course it was personal. I let you in. I talked to you. And how did you repay my kindness? By trying to control me. By calling me *inadequate.*"

She swallowed hard but didn't say anything. She didn't remember exactly what she had written in the article, but he was likely right about her word choice. Inadequate in his relationships with women. Belittled by a domineering mother. Humiliated repeatedly by an equally domineering wife. A victim who sought to fight back by victimizing others. She couldn't deny what she'd written. What she'd written was the truth.

Still gripping her hair with one hand, he reached to his belt with the other. He lowered one lid in a profane wink as he withdrew his knife from its sheath. "I'll show you inadequate, Professor Risa Madsen. I'll make you choke on it."

Panic gripped her like a strong hand.

No. She couldn't let him see her fear. She couldn't let him feel the tremors racking her body. She couldn't let him hear the pounding of her heart. She concentrated on breathing. In and out. In and out. She'd be damned if she'd give him what he wanted.

She'd be damned.

He raised the knife in front of her face. Rain

dripped down the blade, turning red when it hit the remnants of dried blood. He smiled at her, showing his straight, white teeth. "Have you ever gone hunting?"

Her heart pounded double-time. She fought to keep her breathing even.

"No?" He arched a brow. His smile twisted into a sneer. "Well, let me tell you about it. It's like a contest. A contest between man and beast. And the strongest—the most *adequate,* if you will—wins."

Anger welled up inside her. She wasn't going to let him terrorize her. She wasn't going to let him control her. "Go to hell, Kane."

He answered her bravado with a cold smile. "You first, Risa, darling. You first." He untangled his fingers from her hair and released his hold.

She almost gasped with relief. But her relief didn't last long.

Circling one arm around her middle, he pinned her back against his chest. Against the length of his body. He thrust the knife in front of her face, turning it back and forth, raindrops glistening on the blade. "First I cut off your clothes. I like my quarry to be naked."

He fit the sharp edge under the first button of her blouse. With a flick of his wrist, he sliced upward. The button fell to the grass and the fabric parted.

Stiffening, she bit the inside of her cheek to keep herself from crying out. The coppery flavor of blood clogged her throat and almost made her gag.

He sliced off another button. Her blouse fell open

further, revealing the top edge of her black lace bra. "Mmm. You dressed for me. But you should have known I prefer white. Clean, pure white."

Her heart slammed against her ribs. Her breath roared in her ears. She forced herself to swallow the screams rising in her throat. She had to find a way to escape. To catch Kane off guard. She had to. Before her fear swamped her. Before Kane's knife put an end to everything.

He'd gone to great lengths to find the article she'd written for the academic journal. Maybe he would go to equal lengths to read more. "I'm writing a book, Kane. A book about you." Her voice sounded remarkably steady, as if this was an ordinary man she was talking to, an ordinary conversation.

As if he hadn't heard her, he fit the knife under the next button and sliced. The button popped in the air.

Panic gnawed at the slender thread of her self-control. "Even once I'm dead, people will find it. They'll read it."

His mouth twitched. "And why should I care about that?"

"I thought you might want to read it before it was published somewhere."

"You don't get it, do you?" His farm-boy face twisted in disgust. He shook his head slowly. "You don't matter anymore, sweetheart. You can't control things. You're nothing. And when I get done with you, you'll be less than nothing."

He cut off another button. Her blouse gaped open, her bra fully exposed.

She had to get away from him. She couldn't wait until he played out his hunting scenario. Once that happened, it was all over.

Once that happened, she was dead.

Kane licked his thin lips and eyed her bra. He pulled the knife back and craned his neck as if to get a better view. His grip on her arms relaxed slightly.

And that was all she needed.

Coiling all her strength in her legs, she lurched back against him, breaking his grip and sending him sprawling backward onto the lawn. By some miracle, she stayed on her feet, whirled and, in two strides, plunged into the woods.

Raspberry bushes ripped her skin and snagged her blouse. Trees and bushes tore at her face and pulled her hair. Rain pelted her face. She fought on, racing through the woods. Scrambling to put distance between herself and Kane.

His curses split the air like gunshots. Bushes crashed behind her. His footfalls thundered in her ears, even over the pounding of her heart.

Animal panic clawed inside her. She forced her feet to move faster over rain-slick ground. Using her bound hands as a club, she battered brush out of the way as she ran.

He slammed through the brush behind her. Faster. Closer. His fingers clawed at the sleeve of her blouse.

She yanked her arm free, rending the fabric.

He grabbed again. His fingers closed around her flesh. Biting into her arm. Bruising. Holding.

Oh God, he had her.

He yanked her to a stop.

Her feet skidded out from under her.

He held her up, keeping her from falling to the forest's floor. His fingers bruising her arm, he slammed her against the trunk of a tree and pressed his elbow into her back, pinning her.

Rough bark ground into her cheek and chest.

"Who the hell do you think you are?" His guttural growl rasped in her ears. "You're not a person. You're a beast. An inadequate beast. You'll do whatever I say. And when I'm finished with you, you'll know who your master is. Your master is me."

White noise rang in her ears and blotted all thought from her mind.

His hand closed around her throat, he pulled her back against his body. In the corner of her eye, she saw the knife, the wet steel flashing red. He touched the blade to her chest, just below the notch in her collar bone. "And this is how I'm going to do it, Risa. This is how I'm going to cut you." He drew down on the knife, the cold edge slicing into her skin.

A scream erupted from her throat, wild and piercing and raw.

Chapter Fifteen

A scream gashed the air.

Trent's heart catapulted to his throat. He stomped the brake and slammed to a stop behind the black-and-white Kane had stolen from the police station. Throwing open the door, he leaped out and hit the ground running.

He'd called Donatelli. He'd called 911. The FBI and the county sheriff's department were on their way. But he couldn't wait for them. He couldn't wait for anything. He had to save Rees before it was too late.

He didn't even glance at the towering Victorian house—the bed-and-breakfast where he and Rees had made love just last night. Kane wouldn't take her there. Not yet. Not until she was dead. Not until he was ready to exhibit her body in the still-rumpled sheets where she and Trent had made love.

The bastard would never get the chance.

Trent raced across the lawn, the grass slick with

rain. His shoes skidded with each stride, but he managed to keep upright, keep running.

Another scream pierced his ears.

Rees.

The image of Kane's hands on her—his knife cutting her skin, stealing her precious life—throbbed behind his eyes.

No.

His hands broke out in a cold sweat, the grip of his Glock slippery in his fist. He raced in the direction of the scream. When he reached the edge of the woods, he slowed. He couldn't just crash through the trees. He needed to get the drop on Kane. He needed a clear shot. A clear shot so he could take him out without hurting Rees.

He surged into the woods, moving as fast as he dared and as quietly as he could. Thorns ripped at his suit jacket. He tore free and pushed on. Rain mixed with sweat, soaking his hair, dripping into his eyes. He rubbed a hand over his forehead and strained to see through the brush. Through the thick cloak of leaves.

Up ahead he could hear the low tones of Kane's voice. An eerie, almost musical sound. But he couldn't hear Rees. No screams. No soft hum of her voice. Not even whimpers of pain. Where was she?

His heart seized in his chest.

Oh God.

Was he too late? Had it taken him too long to figure

out where Kane had brought her to stage his hunt? Was she already dead?

Panic rang a steady alarm in his ears.

No.

He couldn't lose Rees. He couldn't. She was his light. His hope.

Kane's voice still hummed through the twisted branches of oak and hickory, breaking the quiet patter of rain on leaves.

Drawing a deep breath and holding it, Trent struggled to make sense of the killer's words over the pounding of his pulse. He struggled to hear a sound from Rees. Any sound. Any sign she was still alive.

Nothing. Only the rain. Only Kane's voice.

Damn Kane. Damn him straight to hell.

Anger spiraled through Trent. Blistering anger. Raging anger. If Kane had killed Rees, he wouldn't come out of the forest alive. Trent wouldn't wait for the courts to dispense justice this time.

He held the Glock ready in front of him. Picking his way around trees and through brambles, he raced as quickly and quietly as he could in the direction of Kane's voice. His heart slammed against his ribs, echoing in his ears. His breath chugged from his lungs like a steam engine.

A flash of color cut through the green cloak of leaves. A flash of red.

Rees's blouse.

Heart pounding high in his chest, Trent crept closer.

Kane stood behind Rees, one hand on her throat. One hand holding the knife to her chest. Her blouse hung open, revealing a black lace bra. Blood oozed from a wound on her chest. The son of a bitch had cut her.

But she was *alive.*

Relief pulsed through Trent. He trained the Glock on Kane's head and fingered the trigger. Damn. From this angle, he couldn't get a clear shot. He would have to circle them and pray Kane was too immersed in his fantasy world to hear Trent moving through the brush. He lowered the gun and stepped silently to one side.

Kane raised the knife, pressing the blade against Rees's throat. Glancing up, he looked across the space and straight into Trent's eyes. ''Well, if it isn't the FBI.''

Trent's heart seized. He lifted the gun. ''It's all over, Kane. Let her go.''

Rees's eyes found his. Terror faded from her face, replaced by trust, by faith in him. She expelled a relieved breath.

Kane stared as if he hadn't heard a word. Pupils dilated, his eyes appeared lifeless as a doll's. ''I haven't seen you, Burnell, since you spewed that psychobabble about me in open court.''

''Let her go, and put down the knife.''

Kane shook his head slowly. ''Did you know that there's a vein in the human throat called the jugular? One small slice of a sharp blade, and a person can bleed to death. Very quickly. I'd suggest *you* put down that gun.''

Trent judged the angle. With Kane holding Rees in front of him like a shield, Trent couldn't be sure his shot would hit the mark. He also couldn't be sure the knife against Rees's throat wouldn't do its job. Whether he hit Kane with a bullet or not.

And he couldn't take that chance. He lowered his weapon.

''Toss it to the ground in front of you.''

Trent hesitated. Without his gun, he would be powerless to stop Kane. He was too far away to rush him. By the time he got his hands around the killer's neck, Rees would be dead.

Trent listened for the scream of sirens cutting the air, the hum of cars pulling up the long, twisting driveway. Nothing reached his ears but the steady rhythm of rain hitting leaves.

''Give up the gun, Burnell. Unless you want to see just what I can do with this thing.'' Kane pressed the knife's edge against the tender skin of Rees's throat. A thin line of red coated the length of the blade.

Rees drew in a sharp breath, but she didn't move a muscle.

''Stop.'' Trent held his hands in front of him, the Glock dangling by one finger. Powerless or not, he had to throw down his weapon. He had no other choice. ''Here it is.'' He tossed the gun. It landed with a thunk in a thicket of wild raspberry.

A smile curled Kane's lips. ''That's better. You

know, it's awfully rude of you to interrupt me, Burnell. I've been waiting to hunt this one for a long time.''

Trent's gut clenched. This one. Not Risa. Not a fellow human being. But game to be hunted. A female to avenge himself against. To degrade. To defile. "More agents are on the way, Kane. Along with nearly the entire sheriff's department. Your only chance is to let her go and make a run for it."

Kane cocked his head to the side and smirked at Trent. "Now why would I do that? She's the reason I escaped. I'm not leaving her behind." He looked away from Trent as if dismissing him and stared down at Rees, his eyes shining with a cold gleam.

One slice of the blade and she would be dead. Trent had to keep Kane's attention until backup arrived. He couldn't let him focus on Rees, on finishing what he'd come to do. He took a step toward Kane.

Kane's head shot up. "Stop right there, Burnell."

"How did you plan it, Kane? How were you able to take her right under our noses?" Trent kept his gaze riveted to Kane's face, resisting the temptation to look into Rees's eyes. Eyes that would search his. Eyes wide with trust. Eyes that radiated strength and light.

His heart cramped with yearning. He wanted that light. He needed that light. And he damn well wasn't going to let Kane snuff it out. Where the hell were those sirens? "Just tell me how you did it, Kane."

"Why? Are you writing a book, too?"

Trent didn't react; instead, he kept his face carefully passive. Kane loved to show how clever he was, how he could outsmart the police, the FBI. A tendency Trent was counting on to distract him until backup arrived. "There aren't too many killers who have fooled me in my career, Kane. But you did. How?"

Kane smiled. His eyes crinkled around the edges, but their cold gleam didn't soften. "I just put the ball in play. You all took it from there."

Of course. It was just as Trent had expected. "You let Dixie make that call."

"You don't think I'd leave a spare phone lying around by mistake, do you?"

"And you knew who she would call."

"Big sis, of course." He glanced down at Rees, his face inches from hers. Darting his tongue between thin lips, he ran the tip from her chin to her hairline.

Risa recoiled.

Rage shuddered through Trent. He compressed his hands into fists by his sides. He couldn't let Kane see that he'd gotten under his skin. He had to play it cool until backup arrived. If he didn't, Rees was dead. "But you couldn't have known what would happen after that."

"You flatter yourself. I knew exactly what would happen. You would shut her away somewhere you thought she'd be safe. And then you and your legions in blue would rush in to save the day."

Trent flinched inwardly. Kane was right. He'd shuttled Rees off to the police station because he thought she'd be safer there. Safer away from the action, away from flying bullets, away from *him*. He'd thought he was protecting her, and here he'd put her in danger. He'd played right into Kane's hands.

Kane had profiled *him*.

"You really are predictable, Burnell. All that was left for me to do was kill the few cops at the station and collect my prize." Kane pulled the knife away from Rees's throat and fitted the blade under the lacy bra where the two cups joined. His taunting gaze focused on Trent. "I win."

Like hell. Trent tensed, ready to spring at the killer.

Sirens carried on the still air, their screams faint in the distance.

Kane jerked his head in the sound's direction.

Rees's elbow shot back, slamming into Kane's ribs. The breath left his lungs in a whoosh. He folded in the middle, protecting his ribs from another blow.

She lurched away from him, sprawling to the forest's floor. Out of Kane's grip. Away from his deadly blade. Out of Trent's line of fire.

His gun. Trent lunged forward, falling to his knees in the raspberry bushes. He clawed through the bushes, the thorns tearing his flesh.

Out of the corner of his eye, he saw Rees scramble to her feet just as Kane grabbed for her. His hand closed around her arm.

Abandoning the gun, Trent bolted for them. He slammed into Kane full speed, knocking the killer to the ground, landing on top of him. Pain pierced his side.

Kane pulled the blade back and thrust it at him again.

Trent caught Kane's arm, pulling it back, holding it down. He slammed the killer's arm against the ground, trying to jar the weapon free.

Kane's free hand found his face. Fingers clawed and jabbed his eyes. Trent turned his head, trying to protect himself. Trying to see.

Kane's knife hand slipped in his grip.

Trent's eyes burned. His side ached. Even in the heat of battle, he could feel the sticky wetness soaking his shirt, draining his strength. He had to hold on. He couldn't let Kane work his knife arm free. He couldn't—

A thud sounded near his ear.

Kane's head whipped to the side. Trent saw a flash of movement as Rees's foot drew back again. Careening forward, her boot landed with another thud against Kane's temple.

Kane dropped the knife. His clawing fingers stilled.

Without wasting time, Trent flipped him to his stomach and pinned his hands behind his back. Sirens screamed in the distance, winding their way toward the Lilac Inn.

"I couldn't find the gun. I couldn't— Oh God, you're hurt." Rees fell to her knees beside him.

He turned and looked at her, at the light, the strength in her eyes. It was over. Kane was finished.

They'd defeated him, defeated the evil, defeated the darkness. They'd won.

Together.

A smile crept over his face despite the pain in his side. "Nice kick."

"Let me see your wound." Ignoring his comment, she clawed at his shirt with hands still joined at the wrists with steel cuffs. Pulling the fabric aside, she uncovered the hole in his flesh. "Oh, Trent." Worry laced her words.

He glanced down at the wound, the blood. The cut didn't look good, but he would survive. He had too many things to do to let it be any other way.

"Dixie is all right, Rees. She's safe."

Tears blossomed in Rees's eyes. "Thank God."

He wanted to take her in his arms and tell her it was over. All over. But first he had to make sure Kane wouldn't hurt anyone ever again.

He set his teeth against the pain. Digging his knee into Kane's back, he ran his hands along the killer's sides. His fingers found a small hard object in one pocket. A key. He reached in and retrieved it. "Let me see those cuffs."

Rees stretched her hands toward him.

He unlocked the metal bracelets from around her wrists and placed them on Kane's, cuffing his arms behind his back and around the trunk of a nearby sapling.

The sirens were growing louder now, winding their way up the long twisting driveway. Kane stirred, starting to regain his wits. Too bad. Even if he regained consciousness before Donatelli and his men arrived, he was going nowhere.

Nowhere except to the Supermax prison.

Hands now free, Risa quickly unbuttoned Trent's shirt and pulled it off him. Wadding it into a ball, she held it against the wound in his side and pressed down hard. "Lean back," she ordered. "We need to stop the bleeding."

Trent did as she demanded. They did need to stop the bleeding. And he needed to conserve his strength. Fate had given him another chance. Another chance at life. Another chance at love. Another chance at happiness. And he needed all the strength he could muster to grab that chance and hold on with both hands.

He had only to find the right words. His gaze dropped from her face and landed on the long cut between her breasts marring her perfect skin. His gut clenched, sending pain shooting up his side. "You're hurt. He cut you." He struggled to sit up.

She pushed him back down, flinching with the effort. "It hurts like hell, but I'm okay. It's a shallow cut. Really."

He stretched back and let her apply pressure to his wound again. Dizziness hovered on the edge of his mind. He pushed it back. He wouldn't let anything interrupt what he had to say. "You were right, Rees."

She peered down at him. Worry lined her forehead and clouded her eyes. "Right about what?"

"About all of it." He needed to explain to her. He needed to make her understand. He needed to let her know she could believe this time.

That *he* believed.

He found her hands at his side and covered them with his own. "These past two years I've been letting evil beat me. Bit by bit. Piece by piece."

Cars screeched to a stop in the distance. Shouted orders bounced off the trees.

Drawing a deep breath, Trent pushed on. "First I became obsessed with it. Then I banished everything good from my life. I banished you."

Tears welled in her eyes and caught in her lashes. She opened her mouth to speak.

"Wait. Hear me out. I want to make you understand."

"I do understand."

"Then I want to understand myself. I want to say the words out loud and make it real."

A smile fluttered over her lips and glimmered in her eyes. She swallowed hard and nodded.

"Those two years of living and breathing nothing but darkness and death, I was letting Kane win." His voice hitched. He forced himself to continue. "But no more. I'm not giving in anymore. I'm going to fight. And I need you to help me."

Footfalls echoed through the woods. Dark figures fought through the brambles toward them.

"You make me strong, Rees. Stronger than I could ever be alone."

Tears ran down her cheeks in little streams, mixing with the rain. Tears of joy. Tears of redemption. Tears that washed away his sins and made him whole.

"I love you, Rees. I never stopped loving you, not for a single moment. I love your stubbornness and your vulnerability and that damned light of hope that burns in your soul."

She beamed at him through watery tears. "I love you, too, Trent. And I always will."

He felt the corners of his mouth tilt upward in a smile. A smile that radiated from his heart. His soul. "You saved me, Rees. You made me believe. In light. In hope. And you were right all along. We are stronger together."

Epilogue

"Risa and Trent," the pastor said. Dressed in white robes, he looked down at them and smiled. "If it is your intention to share with each other your joys and sorrows and all that the years will bring, then with your promises bind yourselves to each other as husband and wife."

Risa turned to hand Dixie her bouquet of white roses and lilac blooms. Satin and organza, lace and crinoline rustled around her, drowning out the excited beat of her heart. In all the years she'd loved Trent, all the years she'd wanted to marry him, she'd always focused on the romance of their honeymoon or the bliss of their life together. She'd never given a lot of thought to their wedding. But even if she'd spent most of her life planning the details of this day, it couldn't be more perfect.

And she couldn't be happier.

Turning back to Trent, she looked into his eyes, which twinkled with the same brilliance as the summer sun stretching through the windows of the little country church. He joined his hands with hers.

She breathed in the scent of lilac. Vase after vase filled the church with sweetness. Just as love's sweetness filled Trent's eyes. And her heart.

It seemed so long ago that he had rescued her from Kane's knife, but it was only a few short weeks. The first week Trent had been stuck in the hospital, recovering from the knife wound to his side. A wound that wasn't nearly as serious as it could have been. And Risa had spent every day by his side, doing her own recovering. From the cut on her chest, from her bruises and abrasions, and most of all from the terror of Kane's knife to her throat and his mint-tinged breath fanning her cheek.

And even if neither she nor Trent was completely healed yet, they were on their way. To health. And to a wonderful life together.

She wasn't naive enough to believe she wouldn't carry the scars of what she'd been through. She had only to look down at the healing skin on her chest—the scar the Sabrina neckline of her wedding gown hid from view—to know that recovery—hers, Trent's and Dixie's—would be a long road. But she was equally sure they would make it. Together.

Dryden Kane had lost the battle. And the war. He was safely behind bars at the Supermax prison, and he would never terrorize innocent women again.

Unfortunately, Duane Levens was on his way to serving his own sentence, though not at the Supermax. A sad victim of his own hatred and need for vengeance. And speaking of hatred and vengeance, a card had arrived at Risa's soon-to-be-sold home just yesterday. A generous wedding gift from none other than Sergeant Pete Wiley, along with an apology. His behavior toward her had been nothing personal. He'd been angry at the world and determined to catch Kane.

She pushed Kane and the others from her mind. She wasn't about to waste time thinking about the past on her day. Not when she was marrying the man she loved. The man she had always loved.

"I take you, Risa Madsen, to be my wife," Trent's voice lowered, husky with emotion.

A shiver chased over Risa's skin. Tears obscured her vision. She opened her eyes wide to prevent the drops from winding their way down her cheeks. She couldn't let herself cry. Her makeup would smear, ruining the pictures. And she wanted the photographer to snap lots of pictures. Because she wanted to remember this moment forever.

"To join with you and to share all that is to come."

Dixie sighed audibly from behind her. Single again after having had the marriage to Kane annulled, Dixie reveled in her role as Risa's maid of honor. And she was reveling in the attentions of Police Chief John Rook as well. Although the chief was still weak from his injuries, Risa couldn't help but notice the glow of health in his eyes every time he looked at her sister.

"...to give and to receive, to speak and to listen..."

Trent's voice cut through her thoughts like a laser. His promises to her. His promises for the future. Give and take. Speaking and listening. And she knew that was what their lives would be. That's what they would make them.

"...to inspire and to respond..."

She watched him through misty eyes. Eyes filled with tears of joy. Tears that washed away the hurt and fear and misery. Tears that refreshed, renewed, reclaimed.

The same tears that shone in his.

"...to be loyal to you with my whole life and with all my being, from this time onward."

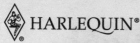

TRUEBLOOD, TEXAS

Coming in February 2002...

HOT ON HIS TRAIL
by
Karen Hughes

Lost:

Her so-called life. After being sheltered by her mother for years, Calley Graham hopes to sign on as a full-time investigator for Finders Keepers.

Found:

One tough trail boss. Matt Radcliffe doesn't have time during his cattle drive for a pesky investigator who insists on dragging him back to Pinto, Texas.

But Calley is one determined woman—so she volunteers as camp cook on Matt's drive, hoping to keep her job...and maybe the cowboy, too!

Finders Keepers: bringing families together

HARLEQUIN®

Makes any time special ®

TBTCNM6

CRIMES OF
Passion

Sometimes Cupid's aim can be deadly.

This Valentine's Day, Worldwide Mystery brings you
four stories of passionate betrayal and deadly crime
in one gripping anthology.

Crimes of Passion features FIRE AND ICE,
NIGHT FLAMES, ST. VALENTINE'S DIAMOND,
and THE LOVEBIRDS by favorite romance authors
Maggie Price and B.J. Daniels,
and top mystery authors Nancy Means Wright
and Jonathan Harrington.

Where red isn't just for roses.

Available January 2002 at your favorite retail outlet.